Fit To be Tied

By

Mildred Riley

Other titles by Author:
Yamilla
Akayna, Sachem's Daughter
Journey's End
Midnight Moon
A Mother's Love
Love Always
No Regrets
Trust in Love
Truly
Bad to the Bone
Meant to Be

Noire Fever is an imprint of Parker Publishing LLC.

Copyright © 2010 by Mildred Riley
Published by Parker Publishing LLC
12523 Limonite Avenue, Suite #440-438
Mira Loma, California 91752
www.parker-publishing.com

This book is a work of fiction. Characters, names, locations, events and incidents (in either a contemporary and/or historical setting) are products of the author's imagination and are being used in an imaginative manner as a part of this work of fiction. Any resemblance to actual events, locations, settings, or persons, living or dead, is entirely coincidental.

ISBN: 9781600430619
First Edition

Manufactured in the United States of America
Cover Design by Jaxadora Designs

Acknowledgements

I am grateful to my family and friends who encouraged and supported me.

And it is with great pleasure that I acknowledge the Roy Wilkins Park Senior Dolphins of the Roy Wilkins Community Center of Queens, New York. These senior women are members of an award winning synchronized swimming team, and my admiration for this beyond measure.

Dedication

To Leticia Peoples: with gratitude and appreciation for being a pioneer by publishing romances with multi-cultural characters.

Let me not to the marriage of true minds
Admit impediments. Love is not love
Which alters when it alterations finds,
Or bends with the remover to remove.
O, no! It is an ever-fixed mark,
That looks on tempests and is never shaken,
It is the star to every wandering bark,
Whose worth's unknown although his height be taken.
Love's not Time's fool though rosy lips and cheeks
Within his bending sickle's compass come,
Love alters not with his brief hours and weeks,
But bears it out even to the edge of doom.
If this be error and upon me proved
I never writ, nor no man ever loved.

William Shakespeare
Sonnet CXVI

FIT TO BE TIED

By

Mildred E. Riley

Chapter One

Newport, Rhode Island 1967

As Winthrop Hatcher expected, he found his mother in the family room. She was knitting something in blue, an afghan for a needy infant, he thought. His mother believed in 'charity and good works,' plus 'to whom much is given, much is expected.'

This particular morning seemed to be no different. In the sunlit room, cheerful rays brought out the high luster of her perfectly groomed blonde hair. She greeted her only child with a warm smile, a smile he knew would vanish when he told her the news he had kept from her these past two weeks of his leave.

Win was a determined young man. He had made a momentous decision that would change his life. His father's brief words of advice echoed in his head.

You'd better tell your mother.

His mother looked up at him. She smiled as he bent forward to kiss her. A small, delicately-boned woman, she nonetheless possessed a tendency to explode in flashes of white-hot temper. Her eyes were a deep sapphire blue which could turn to stone if she was displeased. She demanded and received love and respect from all who knew her. Her son and her husband were no exception.

Win had prepared himself for the inevitable fireworks he knew were in store for him this morning, the last day of his leave. He was determined that Mimi Eliot Hatcher would have to accept his wishes.

"How was the get-together last night?" she wanted to know, referring to the party he'd attended.

"It was good," he told her. "Most all of the old crowd showed up, lot of them married with kids."

"And Katie? She show up?"

"She wasn't there, Mother. Someone said she is living in New York. Many changes in the gang. After all, it's ten years since high school. Understand not many of us are left here in Newport."

It had long been a given that Katie Burbank and Win would someday please both sets of parents by marrying each other. They had dated since high school and college, but after Win's graduation from Annapolis, his decision to finish out his required tour of duty altered those plans and Katie went to Paris to attend art school. From the talk he'd heard last night, she had opened a successful art gallery in New York City. Now stationed in San Diego, Win was a day away from returning after his two weeks leave home.

"Mother…"

"Yes, son, what is it?"

Her warm, loving smile made his heart falter. Would she be this warm and loving when he told her his plans for the future…that did not include Katie?

"Speaking of Katie…we were always close…as friends, and I'll always feel that way towards her, but people change and, well, I've fallen in love with a really wonderful girl in San Diego and I want to marry her. Her name is Mercita. Mercita Mederios."

His mother's eyes widened in disbelief. She dropped her knitting in her lap, leaned back against the floral-colored sofa, her eyes deepening to stoney-black as she glared at her son.

"Whatever are you talking about? In love with a Mexican girl?"

"No, mother, she's an American, born in California…"

"But with a name like Mercita…what's her last name?"

"Mederios. Her father came to this country many years ago. He's a naturalized citizen."

"I don't care if he's a citizen, he's still a foreigner! And you can not marry out of our race! I won't have it! Does your father know about this nonsense?"

"I told him this morning."

"And?" Her eyes flashed with anger.

"He said that I was old enough to know what I wanted. That if I was man enough to make my own decisions, I'd have to live with whatever happened as a result and…that I should tell you…"

She interrupted him, "You've lost your mind, that's what you've done, and you're not going to throw away your life if I have anything to say about it! And I do have plenty to say!"

Win knew that his mother would be even more incensed than she already was if she ever learned that Mercita's mother, now deceased, had been colored.

"Win," she said quietly, "I don't know how you can do this to your father and I! We've given you everything, everything! A good home, a good education. We've always wanted the best for you…"

"Mercita is the best for me," he interrupted in a firm voice.

"That's what you're thinking now, but have you thought about bringing someone like that to this family? A family," she sputtered angrily, almost unable to get the words out, "a family that goes back to the Mayflower? To marry someone of another race? Have you slept with her? And if you have, leave it at that. Don't marry her, don't disgrace the family! Win, please!"

Moved by his mother's tears, Win moved to sit beside her on the sofa. He picked up the afghan she'd been knitting and placed it with the needles still attached onto the sofa table behind them.

"Mother, no, I have not slept with Mercita…not that it's any of your business. I have wanted to, but Mercita does not want to. I love her, so I respect her wishes. I refuse to pressure her. Now, I know being a parent, bringing up a child, is one of the hardest things one has to do, and I want you to know I appreciate all that you and Dad have done for me. I always will. You gave me life. But, Mother, I have to live it my way or it's not a life at all!"

"But, but to bring someone of another race into our family! You can t do that! You come from a long line of naval officers. Your grandfather was an admiral! I won't let you besmirch the Hatcher name! I won't!"

"Mother," Win persisted, "my mind is made up and there is nothing you, Dad, or anyone else can do about it. I'm a man and I know what I want, what's important to me!"

Win reached into his pocket. He handed her a small photo. "This is Mercita, Mother. My beautiful Mercita."

"She's very dark, isn't she?"

"I don't think so," he said. "No more than you are when you tan in the summer…"

"How dare you compare me to a black woman!" She raised her hand to strike him, but he gripped her wrist mid-air.

"Don't, Mother," he said quietly. "Don't. You'll regret it the rest of your life."

Chapter Two

"I would like to speak to Commander Steven Eliot Atwater, please." She was in her bedroom with the door closed.

The crisp masculine voice on the line asked, "And your name?"

"This is Mimi Eliot Hatcher calling from Newport, Rhode Island."

"One moment, please."

Mimi drummed her fingers on the small desk in her bedroom. She prayed silently that her cousin would be in his office, and more than that, would respond favorably to her request.

✿

The seafood restaurant was quite crowded, but Win had managed to slip the maitre' d a hefty tip that afforded them a secluded window spot with ocean views. The evening tide was coming in, and the waves that crashed against the shoreline seemed to Win to match the throbbing beat of his heart. Never had Mercita looked more beautiful. He had not realized how much he had missed her. The two-weeks leave had been both a nightmare and an eye-opener. He could not live without her in his life. He knew it could not be otherwise.

"Mercita,"

She looked at him, acutely aware of the tension in his voice.

"Did you tell them" she wanted to know.

"Yes, I did."

"And?"

Reaching for her hands across the table, his eyes focused directly on hers, he answered her question.

"It makes no difference to me what my parents say. I love you, and I know you love me, and that's all that matters"

"So, they didn't like the idea."

"My dad was half-way agreeable, saying that he hoped I knew what I was doing, but my mother…well, she…"

"Became very upset," Mercita said. "And I can understand, she's your mother and you are a very important part of her."

"You, Mercita, are the most important person in my life. Never, ever forget that!"

"Win," she protested, "I don't want to come between you and your folks. I know how important family can be, especially your mom."

At that moment their waiter appeared with their orders. Mercita had ordered a chicken salad, said she wasn't hungry, but Win said he was ravenous and only steak would do.

The nerves in her stomach were roiling, twisting so horribly that she was almost afraid to eat.

She couldn't help but think of Win's mother, a woman she had never met, who could somehow interfere with, even change, her life.

A mother. Mercita would give anything if only she could have her mother back. She had died when Mercita was sixteen, and that had made it necessary for Mercita's grandmother to ship the grieving young girl off to her father in San Diego.

Mercita continued to toy with her food, aware that Win was watching her.

"What's wrong, Mercita?"

What's wrong? she thought. How can he not know what's wrong?

Loving him the way that she did, how could she tell him that she could not marry him? He was her life, her hero, her other half that made her whole. She knew that. She looked over at him across the table from her, intent on cutting his steak into bite-sized pieces. Each downward stroke of his knife seemed to intensify the spasms of her nervous stomach. Does Win really love me enough to defy his parents? How could she discover the truth of how he really felt? She loves him, but does she trust him?

His blonde hair glowed with healthy perfection, a golden helmet that fitted close to his head. His eyes were an intense cobalt blue. She sensed that despite being seemingly engrossed in his meal, he was watching her.

She saw the worried frown that came over his face.

"Honey, please don't be upset. We're going to be just fine. We're going to get married and no one is going to stop us. We're going to have a beautiful, happy life together. I promise."

Something about the tender manner in which he spoke seemed to calm her, like a warm, fuzzy blanket. She wanted to believe him, but there was a niggling arrow of doubt that kept piercing her thoughts.

Then Win turned her hand, palm side up, and kissed it. The sensation of his warm lips on her skin caused a white-hot flash of heat that melted her resolve. She could not think...not of her future, or even remember her past. The only moment was now, and the only person in her life was Win. She knew she could not ignore the deep need she felt...to be near him, to see him, to feel his skin next to her's, his arms around her, his warm breath near her lips. She was like a lost soul in the wilderness. Only Win could reach her, could save her. Without Win, there was nothing.

❁

"Mercita," Win whispered in her ear, "these last two weeks away from you were pure hell. I could hardly stay in Rhode Island. Every minute away from you was like an eternity! Thought I'd go crazy, nothing there meant anything to me because, my precious Mercita, you weren't there."

They were lying next to each other in Mercita's bedroom. Win's arms held her close, and his mouth was trailing soft, intimate kisses all over her naked body. She trembled with ecstasy, quivered like a taut violin string. There was a quiet peace in the darkened bedroom.

Then it happened. She felt Win's flaming hot, pulsating erection pressed against her thigh. Suddenly she knew it was what she wanted, what she needed, to have this man's love. The only love that would fill and heal the pain in her aching heart.

As they lay quietly, Mercita's thoughts returned to Win's mother. I'm going to lose him because his mother is stronger than I am. But for this moment, at least, he belongs to me.

His second bit of news came later the next morning. Serenely happy in their new-found love, neither of them knew that this information would change their lives.

Mercita's father was expected home soon from his night job, and Win did not want to embarrass Mercita by having to explain his presence there. But he had to tell her about his new assignment.

"Honey," he said, "last night was the most wonderful night of my life. I can't put into words how much I love you."

She looked at him over the rim of her coffee cup. She saw the sincerity in his eyes, his firm mouth that had so teased and excited her body with such exquisite sensations last night that she thought she would die.

"Mercita, love, I didn't want to tell you before, but I'm being sent on a sea tour of duty. It's come at an awful time for us, but I have to go."

"When are you going?" She put her coffee cup down on the table and reached for his hands. She just needed to touch him.

"I'll be leaving in a few days."

"How long will you be gone?"

"Three months," he said. When he saw her eyes widen with shock, he added quickly, "But don't you worry, sweet one, I'll write you every day. And remember this, we're getting married the day I get back! I've already talked to the chaplain, so we can get married here at the base chapel. And while I'm gone, I want you to make all the plans so there will be no delay. I plan to come back here tonight to speak with your dad."

"He would like that, Win, and...so would I."

"I know, honey, and I want everything to be just right for us. I won't settle for anything less. Look, I've got to run, can't be late for roll call."

He kissed her quickly, as if he were afraid he might have difficulty leaving.

She felt his warm lips on hers as he breathed 'love you' and was out of the kitchen door and into his car.

She stood where he left her, not moving until she heard his car roar down the driveway onto the main street.

She went into the bathroom to shower, dress, and get ready for work.

The mirror over the bathroom sink reflected her image. Could her intimate behavior with Win last night be obvious to anyone who saw her today? She remembered the sweet touch of Win's mouth as he made love to her, the exquisite sensations that made her curl in on herself as if to deepen the need she felt. Her father once had warned her, "Don't forget, Mima, you are Metizo. You know, mixed race. Do not be one of the forgotten."

She knew what her father meant, but since the day she first met Win, the tall blonde sailor with his elegant manners, bright engaging smile, had bewitched her. Reluctant to become involved in a relationship that she knew would be doomed, she resisted his attention as long as she could. But she was no match for the singular devotion that Win showed her. After last night, she knew her fate was sealed. She could not live without Winthrop Hatcher.

Chapter Three

Win arrived seven-thirty that night at the Mederios home, a small California style bungalow. He was dressed in his dazzling white naval uniform. Mercita caught her breath when she opened the front door to let him in. Her heart thumped wildly in her chest. Never had he looked more handsome.

"Come in, Win. My dad is out on the patio."

She smiled at him, and in her eyes he saw a wistful look. More than anything in the world, he wanted to reassure her. Before she opened the back door of the kitchen that led to the patio, he brushed aside the lovely black curls that framed her face. He kissed the side of her neck, whispering, "It's going to be fine, don't worry."

He noticed the cheerful blue and white kitchen they passed through. Bright shiny copper cookware hung from a pot rack. Delft china pieces lined open shelves, and Win was impressed, knowing that much of this décor was Mercita's doing. Her talented signature was quite evident.

When he saw the backyard patio, he thought immediately he was seeing a transplanted bit of Mexico. It reminded him of a Spanish-type courtyard.

"Dad, Win is here." Mercita spoke to her father, an average-sized, bronze-skinned middle-aged man who rose quickly from his chair. He dropped the newspaper he had been reading, a Spanish edition, Win noted, and stretched out his hand. Win responded to his host's firm handshake with one of his own.

"Senor, welcome to my home," the man said, indicating that Win take a seat beside the table.

His formal tone did not surprise Win, and he answered in an equally formal manner as he waited for the older man to sit down.

"I thank you very much for receiving me, Senor Mederios."

Mercita asked, "Can I get you something to drink, Win?"

Her father answered, "Bring us coffee, 'Cita, and a bottle of sherry."

"Yes, Dad," and she moved quickly to return to the kitchen.

Win looked around the patio. What he saw was a veritable oasis. Terra cotta pots filled with colorful profusions of flowers. Gardenias, Birds of Paradise, Hibiscus, Camellias, and bamboo trees lined the walls of the courtyard. Dark red stone pavers formed the floor which offered stability to the outdoor room. There were trees and plants that, as a Rhode Island native, Win did not recognize, but he took optimistic pleasure in the setting. Mercita came out of the house carrying a metal tray which she placed on the table between the two men. Win saw two mugs of steaming hot coffee, a silver coffeepot which he thought contained refills, and a small bottle of sherry.

"Thank you, 'Cita. You may leave us now. We shall serve ourselves."

Without a word, Mercita returned to the kitchen, and shut off the coffeemaker. She doubted the men would want more coffee. Then she sat down in one of the kitchen chairs. Her thoughts were on the two men outside. She wondered how her father was going to react to Win's request. Her father knew that she and Win had been seeing each other ever since Mercita had gotten the job in the secretarial pool on the naval base.

Francisco Mederios was a proud man. He was proud of his heritage, followed many of the old customs and traditions and was proud of his only child, his daughter. She knew how proud he was of his American child, had reminded her many times of his pride in her accomplishments. She knew, too, just how much she loved Win. What would she do if her father said no?

As she sat waiting, her thoughts turned to her dead mother, her best friend. If only her mother were alive to share in her joy. If she knew about the overwhelming love Mercita had for the young man who had come into her life. She took a furtive look out of the window. The men sat facing each other, their knees almost touching. She could see that Win was talking, his eyes focused on her father, who appeared to be listening. She saw her father nod his head and Win smiled and shook Francisco's hand. She dropped the edge of the curtain, as if it were aflame.

" 'Cita," she heard her father's voice call. Hurriedly she ran outside to face two smiling men.

Later that night, after her father had left to go to his job, Win told her about the talk he'd had with her dad.

"He warned me, Mercita, that I must never, ever harm you…in any way. That I should love you, honor and respect you and treat you as I would someone of my own race. I told your dad that he need not worry, because I would give my life for you. You are my everything, Mercita, my reason for living; because you are my heart and I want us to be together."

Win's face was flushed beet red from the emotional tension he was feeling. He searched Mercita's face for some sign that she understood the sincerity and depth of his emotions. He drew her close to kiss the top of her head.

For Mercita, the moment was bittersweet. Her father had agreed to their marrying, but a niggling thought in the back of her mind kept rising as a bubble of doubt. She wanted desperately to believe Win, but did he truly love her enough to defy his parents, the racial climate that could keep them apart…but at this moment, as he declared his love for her, she wanted to follow her heart and believe him.

They walked back outside to the patio and sat together on an old but comfortable glider. There were rust spots on its metal arms and back, attesting to its vintage, but colorful floral chintz cushions and pillows made it comfortable, and when Win and Mercita sat down, pushed their feet against the paved stones, they were relaxed by the seductive movement of the old swing.

Win reached for Mercita's hand and drew her close with his left arm around her shoulder. Her hand was warm and soft, which encouraged him to speak. His voice was deep and throaty with emotion.

"Hon," he said. He cleared his throat and started again. "I'm so sorry that I won't be able to get you an engagement ring before I ship out. I know your birthday is in April, and I want you to have the finest diamond I can find, and we'll get it just as soon as I get back."

He pulled a gold watch from his pocket.

"This belonged to my grandfather, who was a naval officer. Served fifty years, and he was given this when he retired." He pointed out the inscription on the back of the watch.

Prescott G. Hatcher, Admiral
Fifty years of Naval Service.

"My dad gave it to me, and someday I want our son to have it."

"It's beautiful," Mercita said. "You're sure you want me to have it?"

"Of course. And every time you look at it, just remember that my heartbeat is keeping time with yours and that Grandad's watch will always keep us together."

Mimi Hatcher received a telegram that night. She had answered the door herself when she saw the messenger come up the front walk. She read it before she joined Win's father in the sunroom.

He looked up from the book he was reading to ask, "What is it, dear?"

"It's from Win. He is leaving his home port for a three-month's cruise detail," she said.

"Well," her husband said, "when you're in the service, you're apt to be sent anywhere, anytime." Then he added, "Might give him time to think over marrying that girl."

"I hope so," Mimi said as she tucked the telegram deep inside her knitting bag. She would destroy it later. Conrad Hatcher would never know the wire really read Mission accomplished, and had been signed, not by Win, but by her cousin, Steven Eliot Atwater, Base Commander.

Mercita was extremely upset. It had been two months since she had had her last menstrual period. She had also been experiencing sickening nausea each morning, which perplexed her. Was it the potato salad she'd eaten at the base cafeteria? She had noticed, too, that certain odors seemed to bother her, especially cigarette smoke and the cloying Evening in Paris perfume that Ellie, one of her co-workers, wore.

But it was Mercita's supervisor one morning who noticed the stark pallor in the girl's face.

"You don't look well at all, my dear. What's wrong? Do you have the flu? There's been a lot of it around lately."

"No, ma'am, I don't think so. I just feel a little sick to my stomach, that's all. Something I ate, I think."

"Well, you should check with your doctor."

Her father's anger came at her fierce and unforgiving.

"I told you! Why, why you make yourself one of the 'forgotten'?" he thundered at her. His face darkened as his blood flushed deep under his swarthy skin. His dark eyes flashed at her with such hot fury that Mercita stepped backwards as if he were going to strike her.

She wished nothing more than to melt into a pool of nothingness to escape his fury.

He threw up his hands. "Mio Dios! I give you home and this, this is your gratitude to me!"

He strode away from her towards the kitchen door that led to the patio, not looking back at his daughter, whose tear-stained face reflected the bewilderment she was feeling. How had this happened? She and Win had been so happy. Win would be back soon and they would get married.

As if reading her mind, her father stopped, paused before opening the screen door to the patio.

"Don't think that navy boy will marry you now! Go back to your gran'ma, slut, whore!" He spat out the words, slammed the door as he left.

Two days later Mercita boarded a Greyhound bus for the five day trip to North Carolina. As the bus carried her farther and farther from Win, she thought, someday I'll have a real family that will love me for who I am and will not shove me aside for a mistake, an error in judgment.

Her grandmother stretched out her arms to welcome her travel-worn granddaughter. She pulled the tearful girl close to her ample body, squeezing her tightly, murmured into her ear, "Welcome home, honey. Everythin's goin' be all right."

"Oh, Gramma, what am I goin' to do-o-o?" Mercita sobbed into the older woman's arms.

"Jes' what every other woman does," her grandmother said. "Goin' keep on with your life. You ain't the first somebody in this predicament an you won't be the last."

Then she asked Mercita, "How many times you sleep with that boy?"

"Only once, Gram."

"And only once was all it took. Well, we got our work cut out for us. We goin' have us a baby…my greatgranbaby, and we'll go on from there."

Go on. The words echoed in Mercita's mind. It was all she could think of, and somehow she knew she'd have to do just that.

Three months later, soon as he was dismissed from the ship, had cleared the post, received permission to leave the base, Win hurried to his quarters, picked up his car keys and drove straight to Mercita's home. He knew she worked until four in the afternoon, and it was now close to six o'clock, so she was sure to be home. He had not taken the time to call her on the phone because he wanted to surprise her. He could hardly wait to see her. The three months had seemed like three years.

The evening traffic proved to be a major handicap as Win negotiated his way on the freeway towards the area of town where Mercita and her father lived.

He turned onto their street and slowed down as he neared their driveway. He could not believe his eyes. Mr. Mederios' car was not in the driveway, and all the windows were closed on this warm evening. All the shades were drawn. He drew in a deep breath, ran to the front door and pounded on it. There was no response. He turned to walk away slowly when he spotted Mr. Akira, the Mederios' next door neighbor.

He ran over to the elderly Japanese man.

"Where are they? The Mederios?"

"Oh, they go away."

"But where?" Win asked.

Mr. Akira shrugged his shoulders as if he did not know.

"One day gone, all gone," he said.

"They just left?"

"Just left. One day, gone," the man repeated.

Back in his quarters, Win telephoned everyone he knew, but no one could give him any more information as to the whereabouts of Mercita or her father. Even the police had no answers.

He thought of Mrs. Osterman, but when he reached Mercita's supervisor, he learned only that one day Mercita did not report for work and her supervisor's attempts to reach her had failed.

For Win this was almost as if the pair had vanished from the earth. He did not know where to look. But one thing he did know…he would never forget Mercita. Never.

Chapter Four

Seventeen years later:

His given name was Raphael Mederios. Sleek black hair, a deep burnished cooper brown skin marked him as a person with an Hispanic heritage. His single mother, herself a product of an African-American mother and a Mexican father, had enrolled her only child in an after school program. He was able to receive a full camp scholarship to Camp Attabury in upstate New York. It was there that Raphael Mederios became Ray Hatcher.

Exposed for the first time in his life to affluent Black kids from New York, Philadelphia, Washington, D.C. and other East Coast cities, Ray was desperate to be like them…to fit in, be one of them. Of course, the fact that many came from well-to-do families, that their parents were physicians, lawyers, college professors, bothered him to a degree. He tried to hide the fact that he had never known his own father. He wasn't sure whether he would say his dad was flying a C-140 in and out of Antarctica, or was a merchant seaman on an extended sea trip. At any rate, when he returned home he informed his mother that he wanted a name change and would only respond to Ray Hatcher from now on.

Stunned by her son's request, Mercita Mederios said that would be okay by her. But she wondered, Hatcher, where had her child decided on that name? Had she somehow allowed his father's name to escape her lips? Had she murmured it in her troubled sleep when she used to dream about the tall blond seaman from Rhode Island who had been stationed in San Diego?

A small boned woman, with a delicate creamy tanned complexion, her long black hair cascading down to her shoulders framed an attractive face with soft features. She had worked at the naval base, subsequently was sought out by many servicemen, but she lost both her heart and her virginity to Winthrop R. Hatcher.

Spiny fingers of fear skittered up and down on her skin, and she knew it was time. She had to tell her child what little she knew about his father, Winthrop Hatcher. Thank God she'd had sense enough to tell her husband about her son's biological father. He'd said it didn't matter to him that the rich white boy "couldn't take Mercita home to meet his momma." He loved 'Mercy,' as he called her. Loved her for who she was, and was proud to be a decent, good father to her son. He concurred with her that she should tell her son what she did know about Win

Hatcher, but to wait until he was older before giving him the watch.

He couldn't remember the last time he'd seen it. Thoughts of negligence, carelessness jumbled around in his brain, knocking about as if trying to reach the area for memory. He shook his head, slapped himself on his forehead as if that physical activity would free his mind and make him remember.

He sat on his bed, reached again for the box where his few meager treasures from childhood lay, now a jumbled mess. He took out his swimming award, won for the four hundred meter butterfly. At camp one summer he had beat those kids from D.C. and New York who'd had swimming lessons from the time they could walk.

He fingered some of his Boy Scout badges. His mother had worked like the proverbial dog to keep him in Scouts. She'd said at the time that she was not surprised when he made Eagle Scout. The badges in his box were crushed, dry, wrinkled scraps of rags and ribbon. Once they had seemed invaluable.

There were a few photos; him with his mother, he towering over her. She was tiny, so he guessed his height, six foot or so, came from his father. He turned the box over, and even though it was empty shook it anyway. Nothing, nada, zip.

His mother called from the kitchen that breakfast was ready. The spicy garlic flavored tantalizing odor of fried Portuguese sausage beckoned him to the kitchen even more urgently than her voice. But he knew he was too disturbed over his loss to eat.

It was gone. He had counted on it to help him find his past, to point the way to the father who had abandoned him, had refused to acknowledge his very existence. He was as lost as a ship without a sail, foundering, trying to stay afloat. The gold watch with fob and chain was his only link to his heritage.

When his mother had given it to him, she had said that his father's dad, his grandfather, had been an admiral. "Maybe one day you can find your dad," she said softly, "with this."

The watch had been inscribed, To Prescott G. Hatcher, Admiral, USN, on his retirement. Fifty years of Naval Service to his country.

When he finally walked into the kitchen, his mother was at her usual spot by the stove, busily waiting on each member of her family. His stepfather's plate was piled with golden mounds of scrambled eggs and sausage, their cholesterol waiting to settle defiantly in his arteries. By contrast his teenaged sister, with the ever struggling 'no-appetite' of a would-be model, had orange juice and a few crackers on her plate.

His mother, spoon in the air, waited for her son's breakfast order.

"Eggs, sausage, cereal?" she asked.

"Just toast and coffee, Ma. Thanks."

She had not missed the distressed look on her son's face. "What's the matter, son? What's wrong?"

He slathered some butter on the toast, bit off a huge piece, and with his mouth full, mumbled, "Can't find Grandfather's watch!"

His mother dropped her cooking spoon and sat down quickly as if her legs had turned to rubber.

"You lost the watch?"

"Can't find it, Ma. Looked everywhere!"

"You sure you looked everywhere?" his sister asked.

"Of course I did. You take it?"

"Me? Why would I want that silly old watch? You're crazy!"

"All's I know is I can't find it," he snapped back at her, somewhat ashamed of his accusation.

"I'll say a prayer to Saint Anthony. He can find anything," his mother said, knowing how much the watch meant to her son. "Don't worry, Ray-Ray, we'll find your granddad's watch."

"This time," his stepfather said, "we'll keep it in a safety deposit box at the bank."

"Thanks, Dad. That's exactly what I'll do…if I find it."

"Think positive thoughts, son. It will turn up," his stepfather said.

Ray realized how fortunate he was to have Alonzo Cooper as a father. But the overwhelming need to find out whose DNA, whose genes he carried forced him to think about his past. If I don't have a past, how can I have a future, he worried. If he ever married, or ever had children, he would never ever abandon them.

When his stepfather had come into his bedroom that morning, it was to tell him that he had a new baby sister.

"Now, Ray, you are a 'big brother!'"

That was the beginning of a deep, abiding relationship between the pair.

Mercita Cooper said she knew the minute the infant Ariadne focused her dark wide eyes on Ray that first morning that there was a special bond forged between them. He was the older, but she became his protector. She watched over him. Even went so far as to decide upon the girls he would date. It wasn't so much that she didn't care for his choices; she just had to make certain they were right for him. She knew all about the unknown father and she did not want Ray to be hurt more than necessary…not if she could help it.

The day the watch was missing, they tore the house upside down. No cabinet, no drawer, no box or basket went unopened. They found old pictures, remnants of cloth for a yet-to-be-made quilt. There were rusty tools, worn shoes, too small sweater, old birthday cards, road maps from family trips, old school papers, plus articles of clothing in the backs of closets that should have gone to the Salvation Army years ago. Each garment's pockets were turned inside out. But no watch. Saint Anthony, despite Mercita's pleas, never led them to its hiding place.

Alonzo Cooper said the whole thing meant that Ray should go on with his life. So Ray decided that he was going into the military. He was still resentful that his real father had abandoned him. But it could be that a few of the admiral's traits may have somehow trickled down to him. He figured that when he needed those characteristics they'd show up.

Chapter Five

Fifteen Years Later

The soil beneath Ray's feet was mucky, slippery, almost sludge, like clay mixed with water. Incessant rhythmic thumps of several mechanical pumps huffed and puffed as they sucked up the dense mixture. Thick, tenacious glop clung to the man's thick boots making it difficult for him, even with both of his very large hands, to maintain his grasp on the snake-like eight inch wide hose. He was a well-developed muscular man whose biceps were almost the size of cantaloupes. But he wrestled doggedly with the heavy hose as the muddy mixture snaked into the waiting trucks to haul it away as landfill.

Huge spotlights illuminated the cavernous area where Ray Hatcher and his crew of four men struggled to feed the huge trucks. Their work area was dank, cold and misty. Sweaty perspiration chilled their bodies even beneath their heavy clothing as it inched annoyingly down their bodies. Their exhaled breaths turned hoary white in the dismal work area.

A loud clanging bell resounded through the subterranean space and Ray spotted the relief crew striding toward him. With efficient dispatch, transfers of the still-disgorging hoses were made between the two crews. Ray and his team took the elevator to the street level where they welcomed sweet fresh air, as well as the caressing warmth of the sun on their faces. They had a half hour of relief before returning to the tunnel's depth.

Despite the rigors of his job, Ray considered himself a lucky man. That morning, as usual, his wife Letty had kissed him goodbye with her send off, "Love you, babe! Come on back home to me. Be safe, hear?"

Thinking about her as he walked to the donut shop for his coffee and Danish, he grinned to himself. He was lucky, all right. Whatever would his life have been like without Letty and the girls?

Eight-year-old Robin and six-year-old Dawn, along with their mother, Letty, were the three people for whom he spent the dreadful hours below the surface of the earth.

That afternoon at three-thirty, like every other afternoon, he clocked out and drove home. He parked his well-worn Toyota in the driveway, saw Letty's Pontiac Grand-Am in the garage. Good, she was home already. He picked up the evening paper that had been tossed on the sidewalk and hurried up the stairs of the front porch. He had just put the key in the lock when a tear-faced Robin opened the door, hurling herself into his arms. Shocked by the frightened look on her face, he asked her, "Honey, what's wrong? What's the matter?"

Trembling, she clung to his legs as he bent forward to hold her close in his arms.

"Momma...Momma won't get up. She's hurt."

Her words were punctuated by gasping hiccups.

"Oh God! Letty won't get up? Letty?"

His feet scarcely touched the stairs as he raced to his wife. He found six-year-old Dawn stroking her mother's shoulder length hair. Letty lay fully clothed, her shoes on the floor at the foot of her bed, and an afghan had been thrown over the lower half of her body. He sank to his knees, saw the blood on her forehead. Instantly he knew she was dead. His voice cracked, "Letty, Letty, oh Letty!" He cradled her in his arms, her dead face lolled against his chest. In his panic state he could hear the girls sobbing.

Suddenly the enormity, the realization of what had happened to his wife engulfed him. He threw back his head; howled with such overwhelming grief his cries filled the room. Letty, his beloved, had been taken from him.

He kissed her lips, smoothed her hair, and gently laid her back on the pillow. With trembling hands, he reached for the telephone on the bedside stand. The restraining order had been worthless. He dialed 911.

Chapter Six

Ariadne Cooper's heels clattered sharply as she raced down the concrete steps of her office building to turn into the direction of the underground garage next door.

She had a lot on her mind. She tucked an annoying loose strand of hair behind her ear. She badly needed a haircut, but where would she find the time? She had never been so busy, not that she minded. She could use the money. There was still much work to do on her little house. But it seemed that every couple seeking a divorce needed her services as a divorce mediator. Her work calendar had few empty slots. But then there was her deepest concern, Zachary. It was certainly apparent to her, at least, that their relationship had been steadily going downhill. And she wasn't sure why. As she hurried to her parked car she made up her mind. Enough was enough. She would confront him tonight. Ask him outright for an explanation. As an arbitrator, she knew that good, honest communication was the key to any successful relationship. And she did not want to lose what she had with Zack.

She thought about what her eyes and ears had been telling her these past few weeks. Always fun loving, ready to try new ideas, see new adventures; she loved those exciting traits she shared with him. And he was the most unselfish, generous person she knew. He always surprised her with unexpected gifts, would smile at her protests.

"Zack, it's not my birthday or anything!"

"And what makes you think you can deny me the pleasure of giving gifts to the woman I love?" he would argue.

"But, please, not so often, Zachary."

"My pleasure," he had whispered as he kissed her cheek.

As she moved about her small kitchen, preparing the Greek salad for their dinner, seasoning the lamb chops which she planned to broil, she thought how changed Zack had become. Moody, distracted. This Zachary Richards, Ph.D., was someone she did not know. Even his physical appearance had changed. Instead of his open warm smile enhanced by his beautiful white teeth, these past few weeks she was more likely to see deep furrows and worry lines creasing his broad forehead. He rarely smiled at all. A tall man with a finely chiseled bronze face, he wore his hair close cropped, which outlined his well-shaped head. To her, he was a handsome man. It pained her to see him the way he was now. Even a weight loss was noticeable, although he made light of it.

"I'm feeling just fine," he would say. "Don't worry about me; I'm just fine…working hard, maybe."

What would she say to him when he came for dinner tonight? How could she get him to open up, tell her what was wrong? Was it something she had said…or done? Would a dialogue of truth separate them or bring them closer? Then she thought about the couple she had seen that afternoon in her office. After twelve years of marriage, and with a divorce pending, they were still amicable towards each other, even during their arbitration session with her. What did the future hold for her and the man she loved?

She had just walked into her bedroom to freshen up when she heard Zack. He had a key to her house.

She called to him, "Come on in, Zack. Be with you in a minute. There's wine chilling in the living room. Help yourself."

When she got to the living room, he had already uncorked the wine and was starting to pour. She indicated with her finger and thumb of her right hand a small amount for herself. He kissed her. She peered at his face, trying not to show the anxiety she felt. She welcomed his kiss. Maybe the evening would turn out well after all.

They settled down on the couch. Ariadne was very proud of her little house. She had acquired the summer cottage, a tiny jewel that nestled among several pine trees beside a lake in a Boston suburb. Hard weekend work, sweat equity, and free labor from friends and family help Ariadne achieve this, especially from her cousin, Jason, and her half brother, Ray. She did not mind the thirty-five mile commute from her snug little home to her office in downtown Boston. Just recently train service had been re-established in the area so she could take the train, especially if she had office work she wanted to complete. She could accomplish a great deal on the comfortable ride into town.

Her living room sparkled with a shiny floor of parquet wood. Colorful oriental area rugs that she had purchased from an antique dealer on Washington Street lent an informal warm feeling to the sparkling sunny room. When she took Zack to her home for the first time, he had remarked, "This place feels to me like a real safe haven." That pleased her.

Zachary sighed, "You know, Ari, I always feel out of harm's way when I'm here in your home."

"That's great, Zack. I hope you'll feel that way forever."

He sighed again, reached for his wineglass from the coffee table.

"Mighty fine wine," he said.

"One of the best from a Napa Valley vineyard," she told him.

He nodded, then confessed, "I know, Ariadne, that I haven't been open and honest with you these past few weeks, and I know I've caused you some concern."

"It's not only concern, Zack," she broke in. "I've been upset because I could sense something has been bothering you and I wanted to help."

He was aware of her concern and wondered how she was going to react to his news.

He replaced his glass on the coffee table, turned to face her, took both her hands in his. She was a beautiful woman with soft brown skin that had such warm, pink tones beneath it that she simply glowed with health and vitality. He looked into her almost obsidian black, slightly slanted eyes that gave her an oriental appearance. What he saw in her eyes was trust. Sleek eyebrows framed her eyes, and her lovely exotic look was enhanced by feathery, sooty eyelashes. High cheekbones gave her face a stunning chiseled appearance. Zack knew he loved Ari, as he called her, and more than anything he knew he had to let her know about the problem he was facing…or risk losing her. He did not want that.

"I'm being sued," he told her simply.

"What for?"

"Long story. One of my patients…well, really I should say one of my former patients." He rubbed Ariadne's hands, noting how cold they were. He understood she was shocked by his news. He spoke slowly and carefully, still reluctant to talk about his problem.

"One of my patients, a twenty-one-year-old college student, had been coming to see me for about a year seeking treatment for bulimia."

"That's when the patient binges and purges?"

"Right. And unfortunately during an episode of vomiting she ingested some material…choked to death."

"How awful!"

"Her family blames me. I had recommended hospitalization, but both parents rejected that. No way was their daughter going to be placed in a 'loony bin'. I stressed to them how fragile their daughter was…needed to be closely monitored, but they said no. Now I'm being sued for malpractice."

"But don't you have malpractice insurance?"

"They…the family…want more than my company will pay. I'm asking my lawyer to try and settle with them."

"Zack, I'm so sorry. No wonder you've been so worried and distracted. I was so afraid it was me…something I'd said or done."

"Honey, no, no, no! Never! With you in my corner, I know I'll get through this. I just didn't want to burden you."

"So what's next? What do you have to do?"

The telephone in her bedroom rang and before she could reach it the answering machine picked up. She heard her brother's voice pleading, "Pick up, please, Ariadne! It's important!" as she walked across the narrow hall to her bedroom.

"Yes, Ray, what is it?"

In the living room, Zachary overheard, "Oh no! That's awful! Yes, I'll come right away!"

Zachary rushed into the room to find Ariadne pale and shaking, the telephone clutched in her hands.

"My brother just found his wife dead! Shot in the head."

Chapter Seven

Zachary drove Ariadne's car to her brother's house in Roxbury.

"I'm so glad you can go with me to Ray's. I would never believe something like this could happen."

"I know, it's awful. Makes my problem seem like small potatoes."

"Oh, Zack, I shouldn't be dragging you into this. You have enough on your plate. God, I don't know what Ray is going to do now."

Zachary glanced over to her. He could see how upset she was feeling. She was twisting a tissue in her hands as if she could reduce the paper into nothing. Life had not been easy for him. His marriage to Letty, however, had become the main focus of his life and now, with her death, her two little girls that he had adopted, how would he cope? The thoughts that swirled through her mind almost overwhelmed her. How could she help him live with this horrible crisis in her life?

"I'm so sorry, Ari. I really am. And you know if there's anything that I can do, anything…" he reached for her hand to give her a reassuring squeeze. His heart twisted with sorrow at the sight of her brave smile.

"Thanks, Zack," she said.

"Don't forget, I mean it."

"I know you do."

There were several police cars in front of her brother's house. Ariadne and Zachary had to identify themselves before the police would allow them to enter. However, they proved to be quite deferential when Zachary said, "I'm Dr. Zachary Richards."

"Right this way," the patrolman said and lifted the yellow tape in front of Ray's house.

Ray and his sister were sitting on the couch with a bewildered daughter on either side, their eyes turning from one adult to the other as if each was trying to understand what was happening to them.

"You think her ex husband Stan Marshall killed Letty?" Ariadne said.

"Who else?" Ray asked.

"He didn't make a fuss when I adopted the girls, but lately he had changed his mind, has been calling wanting to have 'rights' to them, making all kinds of threats. That's why we had a restraining order…"

Ariadne broke in to ask, "What do the police think?"

"Don't know," her brother answered. "Anyway, I have to go to the police station, and if you could just take the girls…"

"Of course."

"They've got their toothbrushes, and pj's and all, packed in their little 'goin' to Grandma's' bags. Right, girls?"

The two little girls nodded their heads.

"You've already called Momma?"

"Yes. She'll be here tomorrow to help you with the girls. Thank God it's the weekend. No school."

A sober faced police officer came into the room, motioned to Ray, indicating that they were ready for him. He kissed each of his daughters before he stood up.

"Go to the car with Dr. Richards," he said. "I'll be over to Auntie's as soon as I can. Remember, I love you," he called out as they left with Zachary.

As soon as they were out of earshot, he voiced his major concern to his sister.

"I'm afraid Marshall may come after them."

"Oh no!"

"Well, he's crazy enough. Look, a restraining order doesn't mean a damn thing to him. Please watch out, I'm depending on you and Momma."

Ariadne reached up to hug her only sibling; a strong, stalwart man whose life had been churned into turbulence by his wife's unexpected death.

She felt his body tremble and she knew his grief was rushing towards anger and revenge.

"We'll take good care of them. And come to my house as soon as you've finished at the police station."

"I will, Sis, and thank Zack, too, for…" his voice broke, "for helping out. Gotta go. Police want to seal up the place."

✿

Ray found himself in the interview room with two detectives at the police station. It was a cold, barren room with a slate gray steel table, matching steel chairs which felt extremely cold to Ray as he took his seat opposite the two police detectives. A single light hanging from the ceiling cast harsh glares against the dark green tiled walls. Ray shivered, the involuntary movement noted by one of the police.

"Wanna cup of coffee?" he asked.

"Yeah, thanks," Ray answered. "Black, please."

Sergeant Jerry Jones, the younger of the two men, left the room, returning with a styrofoam cup of coffee.

"Here you go."

"Thanks."

Ray wrapped both hands around the steaming cup of coffee, comforted slightly by its warmth. He remembered he had not eaten since noon. But as hungry as he was, he doubted he could eat anything. He waited for the older detective to speak. He had already introduced himself as Lieutenant Casper Nathan.

"So," the lieutenant asked, taking a seat across the table from Ray, "you work at the Big Dig?" referring to Boston's new harbor tunnel project.

"Yes, sir, I do," Ray responded. "I've been a 'sand hog' since I graduated from trade school. Worked with heavy equipment in the Army, too."

"Must be tough hard work."

"Get used to it. It's a job. Let's me take care of my family."

"Your wife, did she work, too?"

"Yes, she, she did." His voice faltered a bit, then he went on. "She…liked having her own money even though I made enough…wanted her to stay home."

"And what time did she get home, usually?"

"Three or so. Before the girls got home at three-thirty."

"And you?"

"Most always by four, unless I stopped at the store or did an errand."

"So you can account for your whereabouts from the time you left home for your job until you returned home at four? And that's when you found your wife?"

Obviously disturbed, Ray dropped his face into both hands and muttered, "That son of a bitch!" He raised his head.

'What did you say just now?" the lieutenant asked.

"I said that son of a bitch! Marshall. Stan Marshall. He's the one you should be questioning, not me!"

"And who is Stan Marshall?" the sergeant wanted to know.

"He's my wife's ex, the bastard!"

Chapter Eight

Adriadne was relieved that Zack was with her when they returned to her home. She led the two silent, bewildered girls into the house.

Zachary suggested, "You get them settled upstairs. I'll bring up a tray of soup and crackers, ok? They must be hungry. Aren't you?" he spoke to the girls, who nodded their heads.

Ariadne saw the twin braids of dark hair bounce on each child's shoulder. Although not related to them by blood, her heart ached for them, aware of the painful future they faced. She flashed a smile at them.

"Let's go upstairs and get ready for bed, and then we'll be ready when Zack brings up your soup and crackers."

She tried to sound cheerful for the girls' sake, so over their heads she mouthed a silent thank you to Zack.

"No problem," he mouthed back and waved her towards the stairs.

"At least they have each other," Ariadne told Zachary after the children had fallen asleep. "I'm not at all certain how my brother is going to handle this. Letty and the girls were all he lived for."

"I take it he'll be back here to spend the night," Zack said.

"Yes, the police have yellow plastic tape all over the crime scene. As they explained it to me, the forensics team need maybe a day or two to complete their investigation."

She sighed audibly. Zachary reached for her hand.

"You know I'll do anything I can."

"Thanks, Zack, I know. But you've got your own problems."

"Like I said before, honey, nothing compared to what your brother has to face."

"Mom will be here tomorrow. I know it will help having Mother here."

They finished the meal Ariadne had prepared with such high hopes, and Zachary helped her clean up. He also helped her open the pull out sofa and make up the bed so her brother could bed down when he came.

"I'm going to leave the soup out in case he's hungry," she told Zack. "Doubt that he'll want a full meal. Can nuke this in the microwave if he wants."

Zachary kissed her goodnight.

"Call you in the mornin', see how things are goin'," he said as he waved goodbye and went to his car.

Ariadne stood in her doorway watching Zachary leave. Suddenly she felt vulnerable and alone as the disturbing events of the day began to affect her. She turned to go back inside, watching the red taillights of Zack's car fading into darkness when she thought she saw a flickering light on the lake. It was a moonless night, who would be out on the water? The summer boating season had not started yet. Most boats were still tied up at their slips, still shrouded in heavy tarp or plastic. It was much too early to be boating. She watched for a few more minutes, and then went inside. She hoped Ray would come home soon.

She decided to call the police station. Perhaps they could tell her if her brother had left, or when she could expect him to arrive at her house.

No sooner had she picked up the phone when she heard a car pull onto the gravel driveway. She ran out to greet her brother.

"Ray!" She hugged. "Are you all right? The police…"

"God, Sis," his voice crackled with grief. "What am I goin' to do without Letty? I can't…can't make it without her."

The weary, haggard look on his face aged him. Ariadne thought he looked fifty-five-years-old rather than his thirty-five. She searched her mind, hoping to find some words that would comfort him. She felt totally inadequate in the face of her brother's grief, so she said nothing, just held him.

Finally, he released himself.

"The girls?"

"Sound asleep. They're fine. I have some soup, can heat it for you in the microwave."

"Thanks, I'd like that. Haven't eaten since lunch," he said as they walked into the kitchen.

While she was heating the soup, Ray decided to bring his sister up to date on the rest of the police interview.

"I told them to find Stan, Letty's ex. He's the one who's been harassing us. I told them that we'd even had to take out a restraining order."

"What did they say?" Ariadne asked him as she nibbled on a cracker. She wasn't hungry, just nervous.

"Said they'd check him out, but would check me out, too."

"You?"

"Right. The husband is always the first on the list of suspects, you know. Guess they'll look at my time card at work to see if I was really at the job."

Ariadne didn't say what she was thinking, but wondered who could have gotten into her brother's house and murdered his wife? Did any of the neighbors see anything or anyone? And the boat she'd seen in the darkness on the lake, who was in it and were they checking her house, looking for someone?

Their mother was driving up from Connecticut in the morning, and as soon as everyone was settled, Ariadne decided to do a little checking on her own.

Chapter Nine

A few days later Ariadne drove to her brother's house. The yellow plastic police tape had been removed, and as she walked up onto the front porch of the neat, wooden craftstyle house, she wondered what she might face inside. Involuntarily she shivered. She was either brave or foolish to do this alone. But never one to turn back from any challenge, she put the key Ray had given her in the lock and was about to open the door when she heard someone call.

"Yoo hoo! Yoo hoo! It's me, Mrs. Edwards, next door."

Ariadne turned to see a middle-aged, tiny brown-skinned woman waving at her from the yard next door. She recognized her as her brother's neighbor and sometime babysitter for the girls. She noticed, too, the firm, determined steps the woman took to reach Ariadne on the front porch.

"Oh, hi, Mrs. Edwards. How are you?"

"I'm fine, just fine m'dear, but I am very distressed about your brother's wife."

"We all are," Ariadne said. "We all are. It's been such a shock. And the girls…"

"Oh God, yes, the girls. How are they doing?"

Adriadne's eyes sobered as she responded, "As well as you'd expect. Don't think they realize the enormity of it."

"It's a bit too much for them to handle, I'm sure."

"That's right. My mother is here from Connecticut, and she'll be taking them to school. We hope to keep their schedule much as it was before."

"Good idea. Though God knows it won't be easy for them, not ever again. Not having a mother…" her voice trailed off, then she shook herself as if to remind herself of her original errand.

"You know, dear," she said in a conspiring tone of voice, "the police were over here the other day asking questions, like if I'd seen or heard anything going on next door. I told them no, hadn't seen or heard anything. But you know, I was so excited at the time I forgot all about the man…"

"What man?" Ariadne wanted to know.

"Well, at the time I was thinking of strangers, but then I remembered that I was standing in my living room when I saw Letty drive up from her job at school. It was early for her, which surprised me. Usually she gets home around three. But, anyway, there was a man with her. He was carrying some bags. Grocery bags, I think. Seems as if she knew him because he went into the house with her, so I went about my business."

"So you never told the police any of this?"

"Like I said, I didn't think about it at the time."

Ariadne pressed her brother's neighbor for more information. "Did you know the man? Recognize him?"

"No, don't think I've seen him before. Really didn't get too good a look. He was tall, but not too tall. Maybe five-ten, something like that. Had dark hair…made me think of Harry Belafonte. Should I have told the police? About the man?"

"I think you should. If you want, I will tell them, but they may want to talk with you themselves, either here at your house, or at the station, but they should be told."

After exchanging a few more pleasantries, the two women parted. As she opened the door and went inside, Ariadne wondered what this bit of news might mean to the murder case.

This was truly Letty's house. Her decorating touches were everywhere. The shining windows, decorative plants in the dining room bay window, her daughters' artwork on the refrigerator door, the colorful curtains on the windows throughout the neat, tidy house all spoke of the dead woman.

Letty had worked very hard at two jobs to afford the down payment for the house. When she and Ray married, she added Ray's name to the deed of the house as co-owner and they both decided to remain in the house so as not to create any extra changes in the young girls' lives.

Ariadne was aware that the neighborhood contained many immigrants from the West Indies. Mrs. Edward, for example, was from Jamaica, but several other 'island' people were long time residents.

The master bedroom was on the second floor. Ariadne was glad that the door was closed. Still, she shivered as she made her way to the girls' bedroom.

She found the twin beds carefully made up with matching pink chenille bedspreads, stuffed animals and toys snuggled against the pillows. It was a typical little girls' room.

A small white chest of drawers was where Ariadne looked for clean underwear. Each drawer had been labeled for each child. She found what she wanted, decided to take several changes for each. In the closet she found sweaters, jeans and blouses. Letty had been a good mother, Ariadne thought. Her daughters were well dressed, well mannered, and as she thought about them, were a delight to be around.

She went downstairs to the kitchen. She had promised Zack that she would call him before leaving Ray's house.

"Zack, it's me."

"How are you doing? How are things?" he wanted to know. "The girls…"

"The girls seem to be okay. They seem to want to be together all the time."

"That's natural. Their lives have been so disrupted they have to cling to what they know...what they have. And how is Ray?"

"He's beside himself and blames himself because he did not protect his wife."

"Has he gone back to work?"

"No. The job gave him two weeks of bereavement leave, and he has some vacation time he plans to take. He's crying a lot, which really upsets his daughters. None of us really know how to comfort him. It's all so painful. And I think he's drinking too much. I'm worried."

"Do you think he'd be willing to talk to me? I'd be glad to meet with him, either here in my office or anywhere he'd feel comfortable."

"Oh, Zack, would you?"

"Be no problem, my dear, no problem at all. Sound him out, see how he feels about it. There'll be no charge."

"That's very generous."

"Well, don't you know I'll do anything to make points with the woman I love," he laughed.

"And the woman you love, loves you, and thanks you from the bottom of her heart."

"Ok. We'll get around to the thanking part later," he teased, "besides I have some good news. My malpractice case has been settled!"

"Oh, Zack, I'm so glad!"

"Not half as glad as I am. Boy, what a relief to get that behind me, off my shoulders! I saw nothing but doomsday as far as my career was concerned. But it's over and I'm glad. But how are things with you and your brother? Have the police come up with anything yet?"

"Not too much. Said they pretty much cleared Ray..."

"I would hope so," Zack broke in.

"Yes, and they said that Letty's ex, Stan Marshall, has an alibi that they were able to check out."

"Well, things are making some progress," Zack said. "I'll see you at the funeral tomorrow."

Chapter Ten

Ray, the girls, Ariadne and Mercita returned to the empty house after Letty's burial service, exhausted and drained. The day's events had taken a toll on each of them.

"Let's take care of the girls," Mercita suggested to Ariadne.

"Be right back, Ray," she told her son.

"Okay." It was almost too painful for him to respond at all.

Ariadne and her mother had bathed the girls and put them to bed, they found Ray in the kitchen, sitting head down, at the table.

Mercita had made a pot of fresh coffee. She placed slices of pound cake on the table.

"Eat some cake, Ray. You haven't had much to eat today," she told her son, who shook his head.

"Coffee's all I want," he mumbled.

"Know it's early to think about it," his mother said, "but maybe you should sell the house and find another place. Somewhere you and the girls can start fresh," his mother said.

Again he shook his head. Ariadne looked at him across the table. His eyes were red, his hands clenched around the coffee cup so tightly his knuckles almost protruded through his skin. Although he had shaved that morning, a late evening shadow of his dark beard was visible, adding to his haggard look.

"Momma's right, Ray. I think there's property available right here in Colonial Hills. I'll ask my real estate broker to check. Of course," she added, "it goes without saying that you and the girls are welcome to stay as long as you want."

"Thanks, Sis, but I have to keep them in the same school for now. Maybe later," his voice strained against his sorrowful emotions that seemed to tear at him. "Anyway, thanks for helping."

Mercita watched and listened to her children, pleased that they were taking care of each other. She had raised them that way and was happy that her efforts now proved fruitful. She had another thought which she voiced.

"Ray, If you want to keep the house and keep the girls in their same school, you could look into getting a housekeeper."

"Don't want another woman…"

"I'm not suggesting another woman. Not someone to interfere with your life. But an older, settled, grandmother type to help you with the girls. That's what I'm thinking 'bout."

"Well, maybe."

"Listen to me, son," she said quietly, "I have a very dear friend from

Jamaica. She is very anxious to have her daughter come to live in the States. Now, I know for a fact that her daughter is in her fifties, my friend is in her seventies."

"Like I said, Momma, I'll think about it."

Ray pushed his chair away from the table. "Think I'll take a walk down by the lake."

Both women looked at each other.

"You going to be all right?" his sister asked.

He chuckled briefly, more a hollow sound than a laugh.

"Don't worry, Sis, I'm not going to do myself in, if that's what you mean. I owe it to Letty to find out who killed her and see that justice is done," he said as he went out.

Mercita walked to the door to watch her son move out into the night. A full moon overhead provided enough light to keep him in her sight. She saw him sit down on a large rock at the edge of the water. She saw the glow of a match as he lit a cigarette that told that he had resumed his smoking habit, one that he had given up when he and Letty married five years ago.

Sighing, her somber face showing deep concern for her only son, she turned to her daughter.

"We've got to help him best we can. This has been a mighty bad blow for him. Mighty bad."

"I know, Momma, but what can we do?"

"Besides pray, you mean?"

Ariadne nodded.

"I wonder if the police have any ideas."

"I understand," Ariadne said, "they try to discover as much as they can the first twenty-four hours."

She placed the cups and saucers in the sink and ran hot water over them. "They say that the older a case gets, the harder it is to solve." She squirted liquid soap into the water and began to wash the few dishes they had just used.

Her mother picked up a towel to help dry the dishes.

"If Ray wants to keep the girls in their Roxbury school, he'll have to take them in town every morning when he goes to work. Momma, do you think you can find your way to pick them up after school? And he'll have to give your name to the school principal as a responsible person."

"Oh, that won't bother me. I used to live here for years, remember? I can find my way."

"Maybe you should make a trial run, refresh your memory. There have been a few changes," Ariadne said.

Their brief chore completed, they went into the living room, Mrs. Cooper taking one last look towards the lake. Satisfied that Ray was still there smoking, she sat down in the bentwood rocker.

Ariadne spoke up, "You know, Momma, I'm concerned about the man Mrs. Edwards talked about. I think on Monday I'm going to run on over to the school and see what I can find out from the cafeteria people that Letty had worked with the past few years."

☼

The elementary school cafeteria was empty and quiet when Ariadne followed the school principal into a large room downstairs that doubled as an auditorium as well as a cafeteria.

Carrie Abrams, a young, rather heavyset Black woman, advised Ariadne, "The hungriest, most excited children you will ever see will be coming through those doors in about twenty minutes," she smiled. "So I'm turning you over to Angela. She's in charge and has been here the longest. I think she'll be able to talk with you for ten minutes or so."

The principal made quick introductions.

"Angela, this is Ariadne Cooper, Letty's sister-in-law. She has my permission to ask you a few questions."

Ariadne shook hands with the woman whose warm hands, open friendly smile made her feel as if she were greeting a friend. Dressed in an immaculate white uniform, a hairnet over her short gray hair, Ariadne thought she looked like a typical mother.

"Sure am sorry 'bout what happened to Letty," she said. "And her girls, are they okay?"

"They miss her, don't understand much of what's going on. Asking questions like...when can they go to heaven to visit her. That sort of thing," Ariadne explained. "Thanks for seeing me. I just have a few questions."

"Anything I can do to help. Anything," Angela said and led her visitor to a small office.

Chapter Eleven

"I'm really sorry about Letty," the cafeteria worker repeated as she offered Ariadne a chair in her tidy, neat office and then seated herself behind her desk.

"She was one of our best…could always depend on Letty to be on time…she was a hard worker. I miss her a lot."

"We all do," Ariadne concurred. "We just can't understand who would want to kill her."

"Wonder that myself."

Having been warned that her time with Angela Harris was limited, Ariadne began her inquiry.

"I know you can't spare me much time, so I'll get on with my questions," she said. "Do you have a young man working here that looks a little bit like Harry Belafonte?"

Angela Harris nodded.

"Sure do. That's our cleanup man, Pete Watson. We tease him sometimes, call him 'Day-O'. He resembles a young Harry Belafonte. Funny, though, he hasn't been around lately. But then, he's like that…"

"What do you mean, 'like that'?"

"He's slow. Think they call it 'dull normal'. But when he's here he does his work, and does it well."

"We have two sittings for lunch and he cleans the tables, washes the floors after each sitting. But like I said, sometimes he doesn't show up for work. Then I usually call the group home where he lives to check on him. Most of the time it's just an 'off day,' or 'didn't feel like workin'' today.' Something like that. We don't hassle him because we know he's got his limits. And when he's here, he does good work."

"Have you seen him since Letty died?

"I believe he was here the day we were all notified. He took it hard, was very fond of Letty. She was good with him, patient and kind. I remember him saying, 'Not my frien' Letty! Not Letty, no-o-o!' "

"Can you give me his address? I'd like to ask him a few questions."

"I can't do that, but I'll give you his caseworker's number and she will most likely set up some time for you to meet him. I think he's a ward of the state, something like that."

Armed with a business card with an embossed state seal on it, Ariadne left Angela Harris' office with a sense of hope. She wondered if Pete Watson had been with Letty and why? Would she be allowed to speak to him? And what was Letty's relationship to Pete Watson? Or was there one?

❧

When Ariadne left her office that day around five in the afternoon, she stopped by Ray's house just to see how he was coping.

He let her in, sad-faced and grim.

"Come on in."

"Not going to stay long, Ray. Zack has offered to talk with you…"

Ray broke in, "What do you mean 'talk?' "

"Ray, Ray, Momma and I want to help you. We're worried…"

"I don't care what you say, Ariadne, I'm not going to talk to any shrink…even if he's your boyfriend! All I want is to find the bastard who killed my wife. Stan Marshall!"

"Ray," his sister pleaded, "that's for the police to do! You've got to get yourself together so you can go on with your life. Don't forget, you are the only parent the girls have now. For their sake, at least, talk to Zack. You know," she added gently, "if you keep on like this you may lose your job. Then what? You could lose custody of the girls if the authorities decide you can't provide for them."

Not certain she was saying the right things to her brother, Ariadne hated the sight of her once strong, virile brother reduced now to an extremely distressed, seemingly inadequate man whose deep obsession focused on his wife's killer.

She made one more attempt. She lowered her voice, and in a considerate tone she quietly reminded him, "Letty would want you to carry on. You are the children's father, the only one they know, and they are part of her. Ray, please talk to Zack. If only for their sake."

"But I'm not goin' to his office! Not goin' lay down on no couch…"

"Ray, whatever or whenever you want will be okay with Zachary. I know that."

She watched her brother's face begin to relax as he turned his thoughts to her proposal.

"Do you think he would come out here…to your place?" he asked her.

"Of course he would."

"Well," Ray suggested, "how about down by the lake?"

"Good idea. It's quiet, peaceful, not many people around. There's a nice secluded spot about a hundred yards down the breach, a sort of cove. You'd be private there."

"Thank you, I hope this works." Ray tried to smile. "Have you told them about this Pete Watson guy?"

"Not yet. I plan to see Lieutenant Nathan tomorrow afternoon. Maybe he can talk to him."

Ray hoped so to.

Later that evening after Ray took the girls to soccer practice, Zack came over

"Zack! You're just in time for some strawberry shortcake!"

He kissed her. "Lead me to it."

"Coffee?" she asked.

"Great! I should have called, but I wasn't sure of what time my last patient's session would finish. As it was, the patient rescheduled, so I thought I'd drop by, see how things are going."

"I'm glad you did." She placed the dish of shortcake and a steaming mug of hot coffee on a tray and he followed her into the living room. "I'm going to the police to talk about Pete Watson tomorrow."

"You be careful, Ari. I don't want you to try to find this Watson, it's a job for the police. I know how anxious you are, how upset everybody is…" he raised his fork to point at her as if to emphasize the point he wanted to make.

"Zack, you're right, but I'm so bothered, I just want to know who did this terrible thing, that's all. Want more coffee?"

He held his cup up. "I'm glad Ray has decided to talk with me. I believe I can help." Then he chuckled, "Never mind what my advisor said when I told him I was going to grad school…"

"What did he say?"

"That Black people don't use 'shrinks,' so why would I want to pursue a career that Blacks wouldn't use. Of course," Zack pointed out, "he had no way of knowing that most of my clients are of the other persuasion."

"That same thing happened to me," Ariadne said. "My advisor wanted to know why I didn't go into teaching, 'to help my people,' she said. "I wanted to smack her right in her mouth but I kept my cool, told her law was my choice."

"Your practice is alive and you've done well. I'm proud of you, Ari. You've got beauty and brains."

"Why, thank you, kind sir," she grinned at him.

That seemed to be all he was waiting for. He patted the space beside him on the couch, crooked an inviting finger to her. She moved quickly and joined him.

"As soon as this crisis is over, you and I, Miss Cooper, have some unfinished business of our own that must be attended to with 'all reasonable dispatch'."

"Agreed," she murmured into his chest as he put his arm around her to draw her close to him.

When his lips touched hers, she let herself relax and responded with an eagerness of her own that she had been trying not to acknowledge. But she knew the love she felt for Zachary Richards was real. She wanted this man, needed him to be always at her side. Would the loss of Letty, her, get in the way of her relationship with him? Already it seemed to be hovering in the background, and some inner feeling of impending gloom hung darkly in her mind. She put her arms around Zack to hold him even closer. Despite his reassurances, she was still very worried. Was she doing all she could to help her brother?

Chapter Twelve

Ray's first session with Zachary Richards took place early one evening just as the sun was setting on the western edge of the lake. The previous week the psychologist had scouted the site and had selected what he thought would be an appropriate setting.

Out of view of the house and its occupants, Zachary discovered a small inlet that Ariadne had mentioned where the dark soil of the pond's shore had formed itself into a secluded cove. There were several silver birch trees that leaned protectively over the area, making it into a place of privacy. Zachary noticed how the lake's waves undulated back and forth against the dark beach as if quietly tasting and testing the earth around it. Only if a jet ski or motor boat roared over its surface did it form frothy waves. Otherwise it lapped quietly in the dusky twilight. Zachary felt it would be a good spot, especially since Ray had refused to meet with him in his office.

In his mind Zachary's motives were clear. If he could help Ariadne's brother come to grips with the loss of his wife, get on with his life, Ariadne would not feel so compelled to try to alleviate Ray's problems herself. She could turn her attention to their relationship. It was selfish of him, he knew, but only until the murder was solved and Ray back on his feet could he hope to advance in his involvement with Ray's sister.

His other motive was a professional one. He recognized the challenge to try to relieve another person's suffering. He had been educated to do so, and despite his professor's admonition that Black people don't use 'shrinks,' he felt compelled to help Ray if he could.

That evening, down by the lake, he explained the procedure to Ray, who seemed skeptical of the whole idea.

"Ray, I know you have doubts about this…"

"Only said I'd to it because Ariadne said I might lose the girls…"

"I understand, and I only want to help you to be able to keep them. Here, let's set our chairs down, anywhere you want. Face the lake, face me, back to me, any way you're comfortable."

He watched as Ray unfolded his summer chair to face the lake. He unfolded his own chair to place himself beside Ray and he set the small cooler of water between them.

"There's bottled water in there, Ray. Help yourself anytime."

"Okay." Ray's voice was flat and unemotional.

"Here's what I plan," Zachary explained. "The main idea behind all of this is to help you deal with your loss. It may be painful, no doubt, but I know you've heard 'no pain, no gain'."

Zachary saw a crimson flush flood from Ray's neck to his face, and he knew how deeply injured Ariadne's brother had become.

He turned his chair so that he was seated at a right angle to his patient. He leaned forward, hoping his body language would indicate his sincerity in offering his help. "I want to help you deal with your grief and help you put it in the past, because although I know it will be a part of your life forever and that of the girls', what you must finally focus on, is your life. And, as I said, these talks between us may be painful, but if you can suffer through the pain and agony you will be stronger in the end. Do you understand?"

Ray nodded wordlessly.

"Remember," Zachary advised him, "this is your time. We have forty-five minutes. So now I want you to think about Letty. Talk to her, feel her near you. If you want to cry, do so."

Because he saw glistening tears well up in Ray's troubled face, he added, "It's all right, Ray. Scream, cry, curse, whatever you want to do. Think about Letty. Close your eyes and imagine that she is here with you, on the beach, at this quiet spot by the water. Hold her in your arms, talk to her, anything. You have thirty minutes until I tell you to stop. Say goodbye and let her go."

"Let her go? I can't...I can't. Don't you understand, I can't." Harsh pain echoed in Ray's voice.

"Talk to her now, Ray," Zachary coaxed in a quiet tone. "Tell her you love her..."

Ray's wail of despair ended with cries and gasps. "Letty, Letty, where are you? I need you, Letty, need you!" He sobbed openly, both hands over his face, his upper body shook uncontrollably as he gave vent to his grief.

"Letty, forgive me, but I got to find Stan, make him pay! He's got to pay! Got to!"

Zachary saw a distinct change flood over his patient's face. Ray's eyes glared into the evening twilight and both fists beat on the slender arms of his chair. His hatred toward his wife's ex-husband was apparent. Zachary did not want Ray to shift his focus away from Letty, and he made a mental note of Ray's reactions.

"Remember Letty, Ray. Remember Letty," he repeated softly. "Remember..."

He watched as Ray sat back in his chair, his eyes closed, his bronze colored face wet with tears. Although a big, strapping man, the recent tragedy had left him with a substantial weight loss. It seemed to Zachary that Ray had been reduced to a mere shadow of his former self. Looking at the man, he realized that Ray's physical, as well as his mental health, was in jeopardy. He offered Ray a small bottle of spring water.

"Here, Ray, have some water. I know this experience isn't easy for you. Just relax and think about your wife."

Since the session took place at Ariadne's lakeside house, Ray spent the night at her house.

Ray had come back to the house the evening of the first session, visibly upset, went straight to bed without speaking to anyone.

Adriedne was worried, even more so the next morning when Ray refused to come down to breakfast.

Ariadne was furious. She phoned Zack.

"You get right over here and explain what you've done to my brother!"

"Something's wrong?" Zachary asked.

"Wrong! He's more depressed than ever! Has shut himself up in his room, can't go back to work, mopes around crying, screaming, begging Letty not to leave him, wants her to come back, forgive him. He's got all of us at our wits end...me, my mother, the girls..."

She paused for a breath, and Zachary responded, "I'll be right there."

She met him at the door, her eyes blazing with anger.

"How could you? How could you? Ray is much, much worse! I thought you were going to help him, not hurt him! Didn't they teach you, non nocera primo, first do no harm?" she exploded.

She led him into her living room and they both sat on the sofa. She glared at Zachary.

He hastened to explain, "I should have clarified the treatment protocol so you'd know what to expect, then you would have understood what seems to you to be a set back. But your brother's behavior is not at all atypical in these cases."

"We certainly didn't expect this!"

"You're right, Ari. What I have done is unforgivable. But I was so anxious...to help you...help Ray. I knew how disruptive the situation has been for all of you, and I wanted to help. And in my zeal I made a big mistake. I should have explained the procedure, my expectations, so that you and your mother would understand. As Ray's caregivers, you had a right to know and I should have warned you."

"Warned me?"

"Yes," he held her hand, and as gently as he could explained what he should have told her before the sessions began.

She responded to his touch, concentrating on his voice. His hands still held hers as she felt some of her tension subside. She understood that he had not intended to hurt her, but she was still upset.

"Like I said before, my main purpose was to help Ray because I knew if I did I'd be helping you and the family. I still believe I can help. The grieving process, as you know, consists of several key steps from disbelief, to bargaining with God, to anger, and finally the goal of acceptance. That's the goal I hope to help your brother reach."

"And you have to make him grieve more? I should think you would be trying to diminish his grief," Ariadne said.

"That is part of the process. See, what I want to do is extinguish his grief, replace it with reality which will lead to acceptance and the opportunity to return to a healthy life."

He watched her face to determine if she understood to accepted his reasoning.

"I wanted to flood his mind with the feeling of loss and then replace that with more appropriate healthy behavior. I should have told you to expect the signs of grief to reappear, perhaps even stronger than his original ones. But I am certain that after two or three sessions you will see a more structured, appropriate behavior from your brother."

He waited for a moment, watched her shake her head from side to side in disbelief.

"Would it help," he ventured, "if I gave you some literature on the process?"

She nodded wordlessly.

"I apologize to you and to your mother for 'jumping the gun,' and not clueing you in. I promise to keep you aware of any progress or lack of progress Ray makes from now on."

Ariadne got up from the sofa and walked over to look out the window to the lake. She stood, just staring out for a minute. Finally, she turned to face Zachary.

"Are you sure you can help him? I only agreed to this whole thing because I could see how desperate he was becoming…"

"I do believe I can. I've had patients even more severely disturbed than Ray who have done rather well. Of course, each case is different and no therapist can guarantee results, but I promise you I will not make him worse. I'll stop before I'll let that happen."

"You know, Zack," she hastened to explain, "my brother suffered a severe loss when he was a kid."

"He was abandoned by his biological father before he was born. He never fully recovered from that, even lost the only memento of his father, a gold watch, so you see…"

"Believe me, I understand, and I'm going to do all I can to help."

Chapter Thirteen

She had done as Zachary suggested and read several professional articles that he had given her about the procedure. She discussed the technique with her mother. A few nights after Ariadne had voiced her anger and doubts over her brother's treatment, Zachary met with Ray again.

"Well, from what you tell me," Mercita said to her daughter, "if this 'talking' business helped some folks, we just have to believe it can help Ray."

"I know, Momma. The research literature says it takes a while for the grieving process to burn out. And as long as the person like Ray is obsessed by his loss, he is unable to focus on reality, on the present."

"He's got to come to grips with it somehow." Mercita remembered her own grandmother's advice many years ago, and she had faced reality.

"Zack says he may slip back a time or two. He apologized for not warning us about that. But, Momma, he feels sure Ray can accept Letty's death and face reality. Of course, the fact that she was murdered makes it even harder for him to accept it."

Ariadne finished washing the coffee mugs that she and her mother had used. She stacked the mugs upside down on the sink counter to drain.

"I wonder, Momma, if the police got anything from that Peter Watson guy...the one who worked with Letty?"

"Think they'll tell you?"

"Don't know. Don't suppose they will, but, well," she thought for a moment, "maybe I can ask Mrs. Harris, the cafeteria worker. She might know something."

The next day, instead of going to lunch, Ariadne drove from her office downtown to her nieces' school 'up on the hill' in Roxbury. She found Mrs. Harris in her cafeteria office, having already stopped at the principal's for permission to speak to her.

"Mrs. Harris, Miss Abrams said I could speak with you," she said when she approached the affable woman who was working through the mound of papers on her desk.

"Come on in, Ms. Cooper. Yes, she called to tell me you were on the way down. What can I help you with?"

"It's Peter Watson, your cafeteria worker..."

'Yes, what about Peter?"

"Well, I was wondering if he or his caseworker said anything at all about his interview...with the police, that is."

The cafeteria worker shook her head.

"Knowing Peter as I do, I didn't bring up the interview with him. That is, I could see he was upset, which didn't surprise me, it being way out of the routine of his life, but his caseworker told me what happened."

"Can you tell me?" Ariadne hoped her anxiety was not revealed in her voice, but she was eager to latch on to any information she could regarding Letty's murder.

"She told me that Peter was very nervous, which she expected. Said they were very gentle and understanding. Everything went okay until Peter confessed that he 'loved' Letty."

"Loved her?" Ariadne couldn't keep her surprise out of her voice.

"That's what he said. Mabel Porter said she knew what Peter meant, but because the lieutenant had warned her that she was not to interfere in the questioning, she had to be quiet. But the sergeant seemed to understand. He said, 'You mean you liked her a lot?' Mabel said Peter got all upset. 'I…I loved her! Loved her!' "

Ariadne asked, "Did the police find out what he was doing at Letty's?"

"I think Mabel Porter said something about Letty giving him a ride home and him helping her take some groceries into her house."

"That would account for his being there that day."

"Letty was good like that. Many times she would even take me home, especially when the weather was bad. Otherwise I took the bus. She took Peter home often to his group home on Blue Hill Avenue."

"Letty was a goodhearted person, no doubt of that," Ariadne said. She got up from her chair. "Thanks so much for talking with me. Funny, but I can't see Peter Watson harming my sister-in-law, even if he was maybe the last person to see her alive."

"Amen to that. Peter wouldn't harm a fly. I'd bet on that!"

Ariadne left the school cafeteria, and headed back to her office for a meeting.

Chapter Fourteen

"Well, Ariadne, what does Zack say about Ray? Does he think he's making any progress?" Mercita was preparing for bed and had come into her daughter's room to put her hair up for the night. She placed her paraphernalia, comb, brush, hair clips and a jar of hair pomade on Ariadne's nightstand, sat on the bed and proceeded to take care of her hair.

"Momma, Zack says Ray is maybe a little bit better, but he still has a way to go."

"I've got to be thinking about getting back home," her mother interrupted. "I know I've got bills waiting to be paid. Don't get me wrong," she insisted, "I want to help Ray, but I don't want to…you know, 'mollycoddle' him, either." She brushed her short hair vigorously until her arm got tired. She took a deep breath, reached for her comb and opened the jar of pomade. "And the children…they've got to get back to their own home. Tonight, when I was putting them to bed, Robin asked me when could they go home and when could they go see their mother. It's enough to break your heart. I told them that their Momma was in heaven, and then the little one said, "What bus can we take to go see her?"

"Poor thing."

"What could I say? Told her that the MBTA doesn't have a bus route to heaven. Anyway, the way I see it, the sooner Ray gets his act together, the better. He's not the first somebody to go through something like this, an' he won't be the last. I think I'll stay one more week, don't want to be an enabler…keep him dependent. Didn't raise him that way. Always wanted him to meet life head on." She finished with her hair, put a pink net cap over her head, jumped to her feet. "I'm goin' say good night now, honey, and when you talk to Zack ask him to hurry it up!"

"Okay, Momma, I will. Zack and I have plans for tomorrow night. I'll see what he has to say."

Ariadne hugged her mother, closed her bedroom door, wondering to herself what would Zack have to say about her brother's state of mind?

Ray wiped his damp forehead. He hating coming to the police station and have to talk about Letty's murder.

"Did you buy a gun? The detective asked.

"Yeah," he answered when asked if he had bought the gun.

"Why?" the lieutenant asked.

"Protection."

"Whose protection?" the officer wanted to know.

"Letty's." Ray's voice was low.

"Did she want a gun?"

"No."

"Why did she need protection?"

"Her ex, coming 'round all the time, showin' up!"

"Had he been upsetting your wife?"

At that question Ray's fists were clenched tightly and he glared at his interrogator.

"The bastard was always showin' up, claiming he had rights to the girls, bothering Letty, and threatening legal action...all that stuff."

"So what did you do?"

"Got a restraining order. Lot of good that did. Kept showing up."

"That's when you got the gun?"

"Had to...had to protect my Letty."

"Did you show her how to use it?"

"Wouldn't touch it! Started crying, screaming, so I hid it."

"Where?"

"Top shelf of the closet in my den."

"You mean your small computer room?"

"That's right. Hid it behind a stack of computer books, top shelf. Nobody knew it was hidden back there but me," Ray admitted.

"Well," the lieutenant sighed, "we know somebody found it and used it to kill your wife."

Ray's fist hit the table between him and the police officers. "It was him! Stan Marshall, I tell you! That son of a bitch killed Letty! I know he did!"

The lieutenant shook his head. "He has an airtight alibi. We've checked it out thoroughly. He was in Maine. A man can't be in two places at once."

Ray lowered his face into his hands. "Then who shot Letty?"

"We'll find out sir.

Chapter Fifteen

Their last scheduled meeting was for tonight down by the lake, as usual. Zack realized that this was going to be a very critical session. He had to help Ray understand that it was the 'here and now' that mattered. His wife was gone and he would have to live his life without her.

Zack had helped his client through the grief stages of disbelief and denial. Ray had worked through his deep anger, especially with God, and Zachary knew he had to help him reach the final goal of acceptance tonight or the man could be permanently scarred by the tragedy.

Mrs. Cooper met him when he drove into Ariadne's driveway. She was an attractive woman, and Zack thought Ariadne looked a lot like her mother. When she ages, he thought, she will still be beautiful like her mother is now. "Mrs. Cooper, how are you holding up?" He placed a light kiss on her soft, unlined face.

She responded to his gesture. "Zack, I'm just fine! Anxious to get back to Connecticut. How are you doing with my son? Do you see any improvement?"

"Let me ask you, Mrs. Cooper? Have you noticed any changes?"

"He doesn't cry as much, stays by himself a lot. But what bothers me most is he's alienated himself from the girls, and they're confused. You do know that Ray never knew his real father, took it very hard, and that's why it's so hard to understand why he would not understand how troubling his behavior is to them."

"He's in a great deal of pain, Mrs. Cooper, but he does love the girls, I'm sure of that. I'm going to go ahead down to the lake to set up for our last session."

"Oh, he'll be right along. He just went upstairs to change. Wearing shorts is not a good idea."

"Not by the lake in the evening. I don't think so, ma'am."

He picked up the two folding chairs from the porch and asked Mrs. Cooper to remind her son to bring along the cooler of bottled water and some paper cups.

"Anything else you need?" she asked.

"Your best wishes," Zack said over his shoulder as he walked down the gravel driveway.

"You got it!" she answered, her hands cupped around her mouth as she watched him disappear into the evening twilight.

Beneath the canopy of trees, Zack unfolded the chairs and sat down in one of them. The lake was calm, quiet, only a pair of swans glided by, their elegant, graceful bodies spoke of peace and harmony. A slight breeze stirred murmurs in the trees and Zack sensed a lessening of the tension that had plagued him the past few days. As he sat waiting for Ray, pungent odors from one of Adriadne's neighbor's barbecue grill drifted by. He could hear faint, excited cries from the neighbor's children as they played. A normal life, that's what he hoped for Ariadne's brother and...for Ariadne and himself.

He looked to his right at the sound of footsteps. Ray was lurching along toward him, a cigarette dangling from his lips. He looked worse than ever, thinner, and gaunter; a shadow of a beard darkened his lower jaw.

Zack stood up, took the cooler from Ray. He tried to be matter-of-fact in his tone of voice. "Ray, how are you doing? Good to see you. Have a seat."

"Okay. Ma said when we finish, stop in for coffee."

"I'll do that. Let's get started. This is our last session, Ray, and we have quite a lot to do. The goal tonight is to help you let Letty go."

"Can't," Ray muttered. "Can't let her go!"

"Well, let's see," Zachary said. "Now, like before, I want you to close your eyes and imagine that Letty is here. You will have ten minutes to do that. Then when I tell you the time you have left to be with her, like fifteen minutes, ten minutes, five minutes, and when I count down to the last minute, and when I tell you that Letty has gone, you are to open your eyes and realize that only the two of us are here beside the lake. Do you understand what I'm asking you to do?"

"Guess so."

"Good. Now close your eyes and let Letty come to you."

Close to the end of Ray's session, Zack reminded Ray that he had fifteen minutes to spend visualizing and talking with Letty, as in previous sessions, each session being shorter. He was to close his eyes and concentrate on her. So, Ray closed his eyes, sat back in his chair, and with tears streaming down his face, began talking, asking Letty 'to forgive' him. Between hoarse sobs, Zachary listened as the distraught husband kept begging his wife for forgiveness.

"I'm so sorry, Letty. I didn't mean...didn't mean for you to be killed! God, Letty, not you. N-n-not you! Oh God, not my...my sweet Letty!"

He banged both hands on the arms of his chair, suddenly opening his eyes, glared at Zachary.

"It was to kill Stan! That's why I brought the gun! Don't you see? That's why! I...I...I wanted her to have protection!"

Ray's eyes seemed vacant as he stared at Zachary. It was as if he could barely accept his role in his wife's murder. Zachary handed him a paper cup of water, encouraged him to drink it, which he did. When he had finished, Zachary waited a few minutes until Ray finally looked up at him.

His next words were calm. "Doc, if I hadn't brought that gun home, Letty would be alive. You see that, don't you?"

Zack nodded thoughtfully.

"Where is the gun, Ray?"

"I, I don't know…police can't find it."

Zachary arrived at Ariadne's about seven-thirty the next night. When she met him at the door, he whistled in admiration, twirled her around, causing her black silk gored skirt to swirl around her knees.

"Oh, girl, you sure do look good!"

The white taffeta blouse she was wearing featured a low cut scoop neckline with slender sleeves that ended at her elbows. She wore sheer black hosiery, low sling back pumps, and her only jewelry was a diamond tennis bracelet and diamond studs that sparkled from her earlobes.

He pulled her close and she welcomed his tender kiss. God, she thought, please let me have more nights like this.

He sensed her anxiety and released her reluctantly, saying, "I guess we'd better go, even though I'd rather stay here."

"I'm ready." She picked up a small black purse and slipped its gold chain over her shoulder.

Zachary held his car door open for Ariadne, waited for her to get settled and fasten her seat belt. As he walked around to the driver's side, he considered his promise to Ariadne to keep her informed about her brother's progress…or setbacks

The museum's parking lot was almost filled by the time Zack and Ariadne arrived for the eight o'clock showing.

"Good crowd, I'd say," Zack commented as they joined the art patrons entering the granite stone building.

Ariadne agreed, noting, "Quite a number of people of color came out for this showing, but there's a goodly sprinkling of the other persuasion."

He tucked his hand under her elbow to lead her through the jovial crowd. "I believe, my dear, that they are the stalwart Boston Brahmins who will always maintain their propriety and allegiance to this venerable old institution no matter what is being exhibited."

"You know something, you're right. Isn't it nice, 'you're being allowed an art show in our museum'?" she quipped sarcastically.

"Yeah, right, 'being tolerated,' you mean."

Zachary felt a hand brush his sleeve. He turned quickly to recognize his fraternity brother, Henry Kim.

"Hank! Hank Kim! How are you?"

The two men grasped each other in hearty bear hugs as the moving crowd surged around them. Zachary turned to introduce Ariadne, forgetting for the moment that the two already knew each other.

"Ariadne!" Henry Kim kissed her cheek, "how good it is to see you again! How've you been?"

Still holding Ariadne's hand, he pulled his date to his side for an introduction.

"Lacey, meet Ariadne Cooper, a friend of mine from way back, and my frat brother, Dr. Zachary Richards."

Both Ariadne and Zack shook hands with Hank's attractive young date whose dark curly hair formed appealing ringlets around her face. She wore an elegant white silk suit trimmed with white satin collar and cuffs. Ariadne thought she seemed to be a bit younger than Henry Kim, and she recalled an earlier vague reference to a 'younger' woman when she had been mediating his divorce settlement.

After exchanging a few pleasantries, the two couples parted with promises to 'get together soon'.

Ariadne and Zachary met other friends as they moved from one exhibit to another. They had stopped in front of a huge quilted mandala.

"Look," Ariadne pointed to a printed legend beneath the framed collage of colorful stripes and prints of Kente cloth, "it says here that the mandala is symbolic of the universe. Depicted here is how an Ashanti may have viewed the world."

"Interesting," Zack commented. "It has a certain unrestrained wildness that makes it really exciting."

They moved on to view other displays of wood crafts, sculptured pieces, paintings and photography. Each exhibit presented an African motif.

After an hour, Zachary suggested that perhaps Ariadne had seen enough. He knew that he had, and besides, in the back of his mind was Ray's revelation of the gun. He had to tell her. Somehow client confidentiality would have to be set aside for now. He knew how important such information would seem to Ari. She was so anxious to know who had killed her brother's wife. It went against the grain to do so, yet…he decided to wait.

Zachary drove to a downtown restaurant in Boston well known for its southern down home cuisine.

As he negotiated through the busy traffic on the narrow cow path streets, he said to Ariadne, "I know that soul food isn't all that healthy, but every once in a while I need some red beans and rice and a plate of ribs."

"I know what you mean, Zack. I believe it keeps one grounded to indulge in one's culture. Soul food is a fine way to finish off our African safari tonight." She smiled at him, patted his arm. "So lead on,

MacDuff!" she said cheerfully.

Zack's heart lurched forward at Ariadne's light touch. God, how he loved her, wanted her, needed her…but this ill omened murder stood in the way.

Inside the half full restaurant they were seated by an affable, friendly young waitress, most likely a college student.

She brushed back the long dark braids that dangled around her shoulders and smiled as she handed each a menu.

Zachary smiled back and returned the menu card to her.

"Don't need this, Miss. Already know just what I want to eat. How 'bout you, Ari?"

"What are you having, Zack?" she asked.

He ticked the items off with his fingers and the young woman wrote down the order. "First, red beans an' rice, barbecued ribs, greens, corn bread, candied yams, and a tall glass of sweet tea with lemon."

"Zack!" Ariadne protested, "You're going to eat all that?"

He reached across the table, patted her hand, winked at the smiling waitress, "Watch me!" he said.

"Hope you don't eat like this often. Think of your cholesterol level."

"Tonight's special."

"Well, I will have the ribs, an order of greens and iced tea with lemon," Ariadne said. "And I'd like a garden salad, please."

"Dressing?" the waitress asked, her pencil poised over her order pad.

"The house dressing will be fine, thanks."

After the waitress left, Zachary reached for Ariadne's hand again and gently stroked her fingers.

"It's great to be together like this, Ari,"

"I know. I'm really enjoying myself. Can relax and, well…get my mind…off things," she said.

He knew she had her brother and his problems on her mind. How would she react if he told her about the gun? He sensed her frustration and ached to ease the burden she had assumed. He began to resent his own involvement. Why couldn't Ari's brother have used more reasonable coping mechanisms to deal with his wife's ex-husband? Why resort to a gun?

As if reading his mind, Ariadne suddenly pulled her hand back from beneath his fingers.

"Just how is my brother doing in the talk sessions?" she asked.

"Doing fine, making good progress."

"That's good. My mother is anxious to go home."

"I can understand that."

"She misses her friends, and would like to get back to her own life. I think as soon as she knows Ray has a handle on things and can get to some kind of normal life, she'll be on her way."

The specter of the gun and Ray's involvement with it rose in Zachary's mind. He felt guilty keeping that information from Ari, but if, on the other hand, Ray himself told his sister about the gun it would show how Ray had reconnected to the real world and that was definitely the goal he had always had in mind.

Zack was very concerned. He felt guilty because he was relieved when Ray told him that the police had identified the gun as one he had purchased for Letty's protection. In a way he felt a nagging resentment that he'd involved himself with Ray's problems, but then he'd been so eager to be a tangible support to Ariadne.

Chapter Sixteen

"Ma, you should have seen how awful Ray looked when he came in last night after his session with Zack. But then, maybe, it's just as well that you didn't see him."

"He looked that bad?" Her mother put her coffee cup on the kitchen table where she was drinking her morning coffee, a ritual she and Ariadne had started since her arrival from Connecticut.

"I've never seen him in such a state. Face all screwed up, guess he'd been crying. He was shaking like a leaf...awful!"

Her mother observed her daughter over the rim of her coffee mug.

"You know, honey, it's never ceased to amaze me how ever since you opened your eyes the day you were born and saw your brother, you always were the caregiver."

"Somehow, Momma, I always felt sorry for Ray."

"It wasn't my intention that you would feel sorry for him," her mother replied, rising from her chair to rinse out her mug. "I wanted you two to love each other. True, Ray didn't know his real father, but you both have the same Momma. To me that should count for a whole lot because you know I don't love one of you more than the other."

"I know that, Momma."

She rinsed her own mug out, placed it beside her mother's cup to drain.

"Guess I'm just getting tired. Feel as if my own life's been put on hold. I'm worried about Ray, about how the girls are adjusting. Almost as if I'm waiting for the other shoe to drop, another crisis to deal with."

"Look, honey, somehow Ray's going to come to grips with this thing. Nobody can do it for him. You have to go on with your life, just as I had to go on with mine. No way can either of us live his life for him."

"I guess you're right."

"I know I am," her mother said. "You go on, child. You only get one change at life, make the most of it. We'll just have to pray that Ray gets through this, somehow. My grandma used to say, 'What's to be will be.' "

"Your grandmother was probably right. Well, I've got to get to work, Momma. Got a full schedule, but I should be home by six."

"Have a good day, honey. Don't worry about your brother."

Although Mercita had advised Ariadne not to worry about her brother, her own thoughts were constantly on Ray and his almost unbearable situation. She felt a stunning measure of guilt over Ray's feeling of abandonment, not knowing his biological father. Her husband, Alonze Cooper, had been a wonderful father to Ray, but seemingly the chasm was always there.

What would her life had been like had she and Win had married? Would his parents have accepted her and…their grandson? Mores had changed. The prevailing attitude toward interracial marriages had changed. She had changed. She was no longer a naïve young woman bewildered by the life-changing situation she found herself in thirty-five years ago. Now she was a far cry from the pregnant, inexperienced girl who endured the smelly, arduous train ride from her father's unyielding anger when he sent her way to the practical love and guidance of her grandmother.

She harbored no regrets over giving birth to Ray. Her grandmother Emma was right when she told Mercita, "Every baby born brings love with it, and this one ain't no different. Fact is, he'll be special."

And to Mercita, Ray became more and more 'special'. Looking every day like the man she had loved and…lost so many years ago. So, she did not feel sorry that she gave birth to him, but rather she wanted so much to protect him. She always felt that she owed him somehow, but it was a debt she did not know how to repay. Had she done all she could to prepare him for the life-changing dilemma he faced now?

How could she help him? She worried, should she have told him more about the wonderful qualities of his dad, the man she had loved with all of her being?

When she had given Ray the watch, she had shared the little information Win had given her. At the time, deeply in love, it seemed to be enough. But was it?

At that time the thought of Win's grandfather, the admiral, was merely a phantom, a ghost from the past which gave little for a young boy to grasp.

Mercita walked into Ariadne's living room to stare out of the window at the lake across the front lawn. The lake was calm, with scarcely a ripple on its surface. The trees were standing tall and stalwart, their fresh green leaves sparkling in the morning sunshine.

Mercits longed for peace and quiet in her own life, whatever was left of it.

She believed she had done the best that she could in raising her children. And one thing she knew for certain, they cared about each other. Ariadne was even willing to put aside her own hopes and dreams with Zack if it meant helping her brother.

Mercita sighed as she contemplated the serene view. She still had more work to do for the welfare of her family.

As she stood there gazing at the tranquil scene, she recalled that difficult day. Her son's dark eyes set in a face so like his father's, pleaded with her for answers.

"Why?" Ray had asked. "Why don't I have a dad?"

She had married Alonzo Cooper the year before, was expecting their first child, and Ray was seven years old.

She curled him into her arms. Her heart ached for the slender-boned boy who so resembled Win.

"You do have a father," she said, referring to her husband who always called Ray son.

"But he's not my real-life father!"

It had been Little League and Cub Scouts that had brought the issue to a head. All the other boys had 'real' dads, not step dads. She had made a decision.

"Honey, come with me. I have something to give you."

She took him into the bedroom she shared with her husband.

"Sit on the bed, Ray. I have to find something your 'real-life' father wanted you to have."

She reached into the bottom drawer of a dresser and took out a small box. Joining her son on the side of the bed, she showed him the watch.

"This belonged to your father's grandfather. He gave it to me to keep because he didn't have time to buy me an engagement ring."

"Why?"

"Well, he had to ship out for a three months detail of sea duty. We loved each other very much, and he said that as soon as he came back from sea duty we would get married."

"Well, why didn't you get married?"

Mercita swallowed hard. How could she explain, answer the simple questions of a seven-year-old.

"I truly believe we would have, but neither of us knew that you were coming and when I found out, your father was off in the middle of the Pacific ocean."

She could not tell him about her father's volatile anger because she had never told the child that he had a grandfather living somewhere in Mexico. Some facts she had decided would not help her child, only 'muddy the waters' even more. Through all the years of his growing up, she had tried to provide Ray with survival skills. The testing time was at hand. Would her family survive?

Ariadne went to the downstairs half bathroom to brush her teeth and apply lipstick. Despite what her mother said, she knew she was becoming bone weary, not only to keep up and meet her clients' needs, but having her single life overwhelmed by the presence in her little house of Ray, the girls, and her mother. She longed for relief. When would she be able to get on with her own life? When am I going to have my turn at happiness...with Zachary?

When Ariadne arrived at her office, her secretary told her, "I tried to reach you at home to let you know that the Hadley's had cancelled their nine-thirty appointment for this morning, but your mother said you'd already left."

"Oh, that's okay. Did they reschedule?"

"Yes, they did. Mrs. Hadley said you had asked for some legal documents that they had to get from out of state, and would a week from today be all right? So that's when they'll be coming."

"That's fine," Ariadne told her. "I expect that may be the last session with them."

She took her seat behind her desk and reached for the pile of mail that needed her attention.

"You know, Sara, I'm glad I don't have any appointments this morning."

"Still worried about your brother's problems?"

"Yes, I am, but I'm hoping we're over the worst of it. I believe he's somewhat better." She sighed, slit open the first envelope on top of the mail pile. "At least I hope so."

"Well, I'll get back to work," Sara said. "Need anything?"

"I'm fine, thanks."

"A messenger just left this for you."

"For me? What is it?"

Ariadne moved the mail from her desk, cleared a space, and Sara placed the basket down very carefully.

Slowly, Ariadne folded back the top wings of the covered basket. A sparkling white, colorfully embroidered linen towel covered the inner contents.

"What is this? Looks like food, Sara!"

"It's your breakfast, my dear," came a voice from the open door.

"Zack! You sent this?" Ariadne gasped.

"Indeed I did. Surprised?"

"You know I am. What are you doing here? Why aren't you at your office?"

Zachary kissed her on her check, gave a mock salute in Sara's direction, who grinned back at him. "I have my sources, and when a little bird told me you'd be free this morning, I knew just what to do. So, you're being kidnapped! Get your jacket and your purse. I'll take this," he closed the basket, tucked his arm through the handle and led a speechless Ariadne from her office to his car parked outside.

"We'll be back for the two o'clock appointment," he advised Sara, who was enjoying the whole scene, happy for Ariadne. She liked Zachary and thought the pair made an ideal couple.

"Where we going?" Ariadne asked.

Zachary grinned at her as he tucked the picnic basket into the back seat of the car.

He placed his forefinger against his wide grin to indicate silence.

"Its a big secret, and I hope you'll be happily surprised. But I will tell you this. We're heading south, out of the city. You'll see."

Ariadne fastened her seat belt and sighed deeply.

"Just get me back in time for my two o'clock." She decided to relax and enjoy the morning. How could she not love someone as thoughtful and considerate as this man? She made a promise to herself to push all past anxieties out of her mind. Her mother was right, 'carpe diem,' seize the day. Make the most of it and allow happiness to come into our life. She glanced at Zachary's long and slender brown fingers handling the steering wheel, and she knew this was a man able to handle anything and everything. She sensed he had a special set of events planned. Was she ready?

Chapter Seventeen

Ariadne recognized that the route they were taking was heading towards Cape Cod.

"We're not going to the Cape, are we? Zachary, the traffic will be crazy going over the canal bridge this time of year," she said.

He reached over and patted her on her knee. "I know, but we're turning off soon, heading for Scituate Harbor. Ever been there?"

"As a matter of fact, I have. Had a friend in college who lived there. Nice place."

"Well, I'll tell you, Ari, where we're headed, A patient of mine has a thirty-foot sloop anchored down there in the harbor and..." he looked at her quickly, anxious to see the look on her face when he added, "I'm thinking of buying it!"

"You are? How exciting! Zack, that's great!"

"Think so?"

"I know so. I love being around the water, and I know you do, too. It's so calming and comforting. I can't wait to see it! And this is such a perfect morning."

"Not a cloud in the sky, and to be truthful, I've never seen it so blue."

"I believe it's because we're near the ocean."

"Could be, but," he said as he signaled with his blinker for a left turn, "I've never seen you look lovelier, Ari, than you do this morning." She was wearing a light wool crepe slate gray pants suit. Beneath the short jacket she wore a crisp cotton raspberry colored shirt, open at the neck. Zack was glad when he saw that her shoes were gray leather flats with a tiny silver buckle across the front. The flat shoes would make it easy for her to walk on deck.

He drove skillfully down the narrow winding streets to the harbor and as he did so he figured perhaps he should indicate to Ari that his therapeutic sessions with Ray was concluded.

"Your brother and I have finished our meetings together, Ari. I thought you should know."

"Think he's going to be okay?"

"I do. I believe he has accepted Letty's death, finally, and will be able to get on with his life. He told me that he plans to check with the police in a day or so, see what they have to say, if anything," he added.

"Thanks, Zack, for all your professional help. Mother and I certainly didn't know what to do."

"I had to try to help, Ari. You know that."

He pulled the car into a parking lot adjacent to the harbor. He thought about Ray's involvement with the gun that had killed Letty, but he had promised not to reveal that knowledge to anyone, under the privacy seal of patient therapist confidentiality. Any revelation of that fact would have to come from Ray himself.

Zachary stopped the car where a steel fence separated the parking lot from the water's edge.

"We're here, honey."

"What a lovely spot, Zack! Look at all these boats!"

"Most of the owners have tied them up for the season, but not all. We've only got a little way to walk to the sloop. Here, let me get the basket, and I have a blanket, too. Better keep your jacket on. Sometimes it's breezy on the water. There she is!"

Ariadne gasped with delight at the sight of the magnificent sleek boat of teak and mahogany. Its hull was blazing white, its blue sails tied down as it lay anchored in the deep blue-green water that seemed to caress it with care. The boat seemed to offer a spirit of peace and tranquility that Ariadne felt she could soak up like a proverbial sponge. The open deck with a shining steel and wood steering wheel welcomed Zack and Ariadne, and from there Zack led her to the main salon, an invitingly lovely space with books, gracious art and bunks on either side of a blonde, handcrafted wooden table.

Zack placed the picnic basket on the table.

"The galley is up ahead and a few steps beyond is the bathroom, Ari," he told her, "but on the boat it's called the 'head'."

"Just might take a look at that," she said as she moved forward to the area Zack pointed out to her.

When she returned, he had set the table. Tall candles in the center with a glass bowl of fresh yellow chrysanthemums, rosy-pink asters and large elegant dahlia blossoms of a deep ruby red color intertwined with the glowing white candles.

Zack had opened a thermos and poured golden mimosas into two glasses. He pointed to one of the side bunks for Ariadne to sit, and he offered her a frosted glass.

"Here's to us, Ari. May all of our tomorrows bring smooth sailing."

"Hear, hear. I'll agree to that, Zack."

She sipped her drink and watched with amused delight as Zack laid out her 'breakfast'. More like a brunch, she thought. She spread a linen napkin over her lap.

The fresh fruit plate that he offered first was filled with sugar glazed green grapes, cubes of cantaloupe and honeydew melon, huge succulent red strawberries with crème fraiches.

"This fruit is delicious, Zack. How did you keep it so cold?"

He showed her a small line zippered bag with frozen ice containers in it.

"All in knowing how, my dear," he smiled, pleased that she seemed happy.

"You're a genius, and you know it," she teased.

He sat beside her with his own plate of food while the boat rocked gently back and forth on the water.

"Taste good?" he asked.

"Um-m, heavenly," she answered as she skewered a golden globe of juicy cantaloupe and popped it into her mouth.

"There's more in that basket, you know," he pointed out to her.

"More?"

"Sure, more."

He reached in and brought out a plastic covered plate which he handed to her. When she uncovered the small plate, she gasped. Tiny finger sandwiches were placed around a lettuce leaf with glistening moist mushrooms, black olives, carrot sticks and thinly sliced cucumbers arrayed on the pale green lettuce.

"Zack, how beautiful! Now I know for a fact you didn't do all of this by yourself!"

She could see tiny bits of pink lobster meat feathering out of the thin sandwich bread.

"And even lobster! Zack, you're too much!"

"I just want to make you happy, sweetheart."

He looked at her to be sure she understood what he meant.

"Well, you've certainly made today one I'll remember, that's for sure."

From the seemingly bottomless basket he retrieved a thermos of coffee and two cerulean blue ceramic mugs. He poured coffee for her in the mug labeled Heroine and another cup for himself labeled Hero. Ariadne laughed when she saw them.

Then he went over to a corner of the salon to turn on a battery run stereo, and the duet Unforgettable by Nat 'King' Cole and his daughter, Natalie, filled the comfortable space with an atmosphere of tranquil peace. Just what Zachary was hoping to achieve. He'd never seen Ariadne look so lovely, and so much at ease. He hoped her difficult days with her family were behind her and that he could ask her to marry him. Would he be lucky enough to do it today? Did she realize how much he loved her? As the song ended, he hoped it was time to act. The box in his coat pocket was crying out to him. Do it! Do it now!

Ariadne finished her coffee and glanced at her watch. Zack felt even more pressure to act.

"I know it's getting close to noon. We'll start back as soon as I pack up," he said.

"I'll help."

"No, indeed not! I want you to relax and enjoy every minute of this."

Quickly he gathered up the remnants of their brunch and rather efficiently, too, Ariadne thought as she watched.

"I'll take this out to the car and come back for you. We have a few more minutes. Don't worry, I'll get you back on time."

When he returned, Ariadne was sitting out on the deck, looking over the water. He stood quietly for a full minute watching the woman he loved, the most caring person he had ever known. She was smart, hardworking, and for some unknown reason was able to bring out the best in him, make him feel privileged to know and love her. He wanted desperately to hold her, never let her go. He wanted her to be his wife, partner, lover. An inner voice said, Now!

He placed his foot on the deck and his weight rocked the boat, causing Ariadne to look at him, her mouth slightly opened as if to speak.

She was so beautiful, he thought. Her dark eyes widened as he came close to where she was sitting. The sun had warmed her skin so that it glowed with health and vitality. The gentle sea breeze had misted her dark hair into bewitching tendrils that curled around her lovely face.

The moment had come and Zachary knew it. Ariadne's eyes widened as he got down on one knee and took both her hands in his.

"Zack?"

"Ari," he plunged ahead, still holding both her hands, caressing her knuckles with his thumbs as if afraid to let go.

He cleared his throat, swallowed and cleared his throat again with a nervous cough.

"Ari, honey, you do know how much I love you, since the day Henry introduced us. I've wanted for so long to make a commitment, but, well, with all that's been going on, but I can't wait a minute more!"

Deep emotions flickered across his face and Ariadne saw tears in his eyes. His love for her almost rendered her speechless, and her own eyes moistened.

"Say you love me, Ari. Say you'll marry me, please," he begged.

He let go of her hands and brought out the box from his pocket. He looked into her eyes, waiting for her response.

He was still holding the box, but she took his face in both of her hands. With a steady, unblinking gaze, she answered, "Yes, Zack, I will marry you! Yes, yes!" she emphasized.

With trembling hands, Zachary struggled to put the diamond solitaire on her finger. Then still on his knees, he kissed her. At that moment the

Scituate Harbor Master sailed by. Zack saw him, jumped to his feet and yelled across the span of water, his hands cupped around his mouth, "She said yes!"

The Harbormaster blew the boat's horn and waved, yelling back, "Congratulations!"

Chapter Eighteen

A few days later Ray received a call from Sergeant Jones. "Glad you came in, Mr. Hatcher," he said agreeably and shook hands with Ray. "We were about to call you to ask a few questions."

"About the gun," Ray offered.

"That's right." The lieutenant explained, "The gun was found in a sewer catch basin not too far from your house. It was dropped there. Peter Watson dropped the gun. We know, too, that the gun was registered to you. We've already checked that much out."

"That's right, lieutenant. I bought the gun for my wife for…" his voice lowered a bit and he struggled for a moment before continuing, "for her protection. You see," he raised his head, looked directly at the officer before continuing in a firm voice, "her ex-husband, the bastard, had been bothering her. I'd even taken out a restraining order."

"We know about that, sir," the lieutenant's voice was steady, his gaze direct as he explained the situation to Ray.

"Forensics has examined the gun and found two sets of prints, yours and…"

Ray nearly rose from his chair. "Whose?"

The officer raised his hand in a restraining manner. "They belong to Pete Watson, but he'd been cleared and we're beginning to think that your wife's death was an accidental one."

"How do you know? Peter Watson…doesn't he have some kind of mental defect?" Ray wanted to know.

"We questioned him at length, Mr. Hatcher, and we're satisfied with his answers. Your wife's shooting was an accident. The forensic evidence uncovered at the scene corroborates, bears out our conclusion that Mrs. Hatcher's death was an unfortunate accident. In legal terms, homicide per unfortunium, where a person is doing a lawful act and without any malice aforethought or intention to harm unfortunately kills another person. This is sometimes called an excusable homicide."

Angry tears filled Ray's eyes as he glared at the police officer.

"So, you're 'excusing' him for my wife's death?"

Lieutenant Nathan opened his hands across his desk in a gesture of surrender.

"Everyone…including you, sir."

"Me?"

"Afraid so. Let me go over the scenario as we have put it together. What I'm about to tell you is what we already know to be factual.

"One, you brought the gun into your home. Your wife was upset so you put it on the top shelf of a cabinet in your small computer room.

That correct so far?"

"Yes. No one knew it was there but me."

"Right. We also found out that Mrs. Hatcher would sometimes drive Peter Watson to his group home from the school where they both worked."

"Sometimes she did. He was a good kid, I guess, just slow."

"That's right. Now Mrs. Edwards, your next door neighbor, positively identified him as the person she saw go into your house with your wife..."

"You mean Pete accidentally killed Letty?"

"Not the way you're thinking."

"Well, how?"

"It appears Mrs. Hatcher took Peter to the computer room. She knew he was interested in them..."

"Yeah, she mentioned that more than once to me."

"Evidently she suggested that Pete get the computer books down from the cabinet shelf, and when he did so the gun fell to the floor. The safety was off and it fired."

At that moment Ray dropped his head into his hands, but the lieutenant continued to speak in a matter-of-fact voice.

"Forensics traced the bullet's trajectory path to the upper window frame through to the victim's head, and that same bullet was found imbedded in the opposite wall."

"How did she...end up on her bed?"

"Peter put her there. He knew something was wrong with her, said he took the 'bad' gun that had hurt his friend and dropped it in the catch basin where we found it, like I told you."

"It's all my fault." Ray slammed his fist several times on the arm of his chair.

The lieutenant observed Ray closely, recognizing the enormity of the man's pain. He waited until he felt that Ray had gained some control over his emotions after the stunning news he had just received. He rose from his seat at his desk, poured a cup of coffee for Ray and placed it on the desk.

"Need sugar, cream?" he asked.

"No, just black will do. Thanks."

The policeman pushed an open box of tissues closer to Ray, who took a couple, mumbled, "Thanks," and wiped his eyes. He took a sip of the hot coffee and appealed to the lieutenant, "Now what?"

The lieutenant explained in a calm voice the next step he would take.

"I'd like a signed statement from you concerning your possession of the gun. You know, just what you told me this morning, and a written report signed by me and my sergeant will be forwarded to the District

Attorney. I don't believe he will disagree with our conclusion. As I said, it was an unfortunate accident and I think he will rule it as such. My advice to you, sir, is to pick up the pieces and go on with your life. I understand there are two little girls involved…"

"My wife's, but I have legal custody."

"Good. I know you'll do your best by them." Then he added as he walked a shaken Ray to the door, "Don't think there'll be any more consequences to this terrible accident, at least I believe the D.A. will view it like that. Is there anything I can do for you?"

"No, sir…I…I don't think so."

"Well, try to get your life back on track. Planning to go back to work?"

"Very soon. I've used up most of my time."

"If there is anything we can do to help, let us know."

The two men shook hands and Ray left.

Still stricken but somewhat relieved, Ray left the police station. Some of the guilt stayed with him. If he had not brought the gun to his home, his Letty would be alive. It was a terrible accident, and he would have to live with it.

Chapter Nineteen

Three months had passed and Mercita returned to Connecticut to resume her life.

"You know, Ariadne, that these past few months have been the happiest I've had in years. You and Zachary getting married, and Ray's doing so much better."

"I know what you mean, Momma," her daughter answered.

Her mother's cheerful bright voice rang over the lines from Connecticut and Ariadne could picture her mother, impeccably groomed, having just returned from her synchronized swimming class, nails done, hair carefully coifed, dressed for lunch with one of her friends for an afternoon of serene relaxation.

Her mother was an unmistakably different woman from the African-American, half-Mexican young woman abandoned by her lover so many years before. She had turned her back on those fearful days, had rebuilt her life with hard work and determination. She rebuilt a happy life with Alonzo Cooper, rarely ever speaking of her difficult times. Fiercely proud of herself and her family, if she ever thought about her son's biological father, she never mentioned it. She was stubbornly proud of her family.

Ariadne knew her mother was excited over her upcoming marriage to Zachary and was extremely pleased over Ray's excellent progress in handling his tragic loss.

The conversation had taken place a few days prior to her departure to her home in Connecticut. As usual, it was over their morning coffee ritual.

"Your Zachary is a genius. He sure put your brother on the right track. And I know how much Ray suffered, all that guilt for having the gun in the house in the first place."

"Zachary wanted so much to help Ray. I think the fact that the District Attorney decided not to press criminal charges helped a great deal, saying there was no criminal liability."

A spastic shiver went through her body as she continued to sip her coffee that late summer morning. Ariadne thought about the horrendous summer months they had all endured. She sighed and changed the subject.

"Let me bring you up to date on our wedding plans."

"Great! I'd love to hear what you two have decided."

"We're trying to find a reception hall near the ocean, perhaps down on the south shore. And we've asked Father Kempton…"

"You mean our old friend from St. Gregory's?" her mother interrupted with excited pleasure. "Isn't he retired now?" she asked.

"He is. But, Momma, he said he would come out of retirement to officiate…that I'd better not dream of having anyone else."

"Just like Father Kempton."

"Said that we were more than parishioners, we were family."

"Sounds like Father. And, of course, you know that when my time comes I want him to be sending me on my last journey."

"God, Momma! Don't talk like that! Haven't we been through enough this summer?"

Without acknowledging that she may have upset her daughter with her sobering remarks about death, Mercita Cooper continued her questions about the wedding plans.

"Listen, honey, I'd love to help you pick out your wedding gown. I have an idea…"

"Yes, Momma?"

"Think you could come down for a weekend? We could take the train to New York and see what's available."

"Don't see why not. Sounds like a good idea to me. How about Thanksgiving weekend? Ray plans to take the girls to Disney World…says he thinks it best to start a new holiday tradition now that Letty is gone. He told me he got the idea from Zack."

"That idea makes a whole lot of sense to me," her mother responded.

"I think so, too, and that homemaker, you know, your friend's daughter from Jamaica, Mrs. Francis, seems to fit in fine. The girls love her, and Ray is comfortable leaving the girls in her care. And, Momma, you know what," Ariadne chuckled over the telephone, "that lady's West Indian cooking is putting weight back on your son."

"Sure am glad to hear that. Is he going to work everyday?"

"Yes, he is. Thinking about going to night school to work on his computer skills. Says he'd like to get in a different line of work."

"I'd like to see him do just that," her mother agreed. "That tunnel work is so dangerous. I know the money is good, but it's so dangerous."

"And stressful, too," Ariadne added. She looked at her watch to check the time. She had a busy day ahead with several clients and she was having dinner with Zachary later. She knew her mother would talk a good while longer, so she decided she'd better hang up.

"Mom, I've got to go."

"All right. Call me when you decide on our weekend."

"I'll do that. You're feeling okay, right?"

"Never felt better, my dear. Looking forward to our weekend. Maybe we can take in a Broadway show."

"Sounds good, but we can't try to do too much. Let's see how it goes. I do want to look for a wedding gift, a memento for Zack. Maybe you can help me with that."

"Love to," her mother said.

After their goodbyes were said, Ariadne sat by the phone for a few moments, her mother's cheerful, enthusiastic voice ringing in her ears. God alone knew how much cheering up she needed, despite her upcoming marriage. The ever-present cloud hanging over her grew darker each day. Her brother was not the only family member with a burden to bear. Could Zack, would Zack understand and help her as he had helped Ray? Did he love her enough to do so? Although not a grievous situation like her brother's, it was still a life-altering condition that she had pushed far back into her mind. But like murky waters of a dank swamp, it would bubble up through her consciousness threatening to disturb the serene life she had hoped to find with the man she loved.

When she arrived at her office that morning, Sara Young had organized her day's work very well, with the Hadley's due in at ten-thirty that morning for their last meeting. The final papers would be signed and hopefully they would go forward to an amicable divorce and satisfactory single lives.

The next couple she was scheduled to see were the most severely mismatched couple she ever interviewed. She was twenty and he was twenty-two. Ariadne was quick to decide that no matter what she suggested, the misunderstandings and blame lying between the pair would be too difficult to overcome. They were like two bratty children fighting over a toy.

Her first suggestion that they divide their assets equitably and go on to get the divorce and move on fell on, deaf ears.

"I'm afraid I can't help you," she told them. "I'm very sorry. Please see my secretary on your way out. You'll only be charged for today's consultation."

She shook hands with each of them, then walked them to her office door.

"Sara," she said, "the charge is only for today's visit. No further appointments."

'Yes, ma'am."

Ariadne closed her office door and sank into her chair behind her desk. The self-centered behavior she had just witnessed reminded her that truth and honesty should be the first considerations in a successful relationship. Without those principles, failure loomed. Could she risk that?

Chapter Twenty

Ariadne's heels tapped sharply on the sidewalk as she went to her car parked in the underground garage, each step punctuated by an echo in her head, tell him, tell him. But her mind repeated, I can't , I can't, I can't.

She thought she had pushed the incident so deep inside her consciousness, it need never be considered again. But lately it seemed the nearer her wedding day approached, the stronger the 'incident' intruded into her present.

On this particular evening she and Zachary planned to select wedding invitations from the printer's sample book, make a final decision on the caterer and the menu to be served, and determine where they would live after marriage.

She arrived at her home in time to shower and change.

She prepared a simple meal of spaghetti and meatballs, a freshly tossed salad to be served with crusty French rolls. She put together a fresh fruit compote and had purchased thin ginger snaps to accompany it. As she worked in her small kitchen she knew that tonight would prove to be the most pivotal night of her life. Did Zachary love her enough…to marry her when he learned the truth?

Promptly at six-thirty Ariadne heard Zachary's key in the door. She went to greet him, and despite her prior misgivings, felt reassured when she saw his smiling face.

"Here I am, wife-to-be," he announced in a cheerful voice.

He swept her up in a warm, enfolding embrace that she welcomed. She needed his strength, his commitment, his love as much as she needed air to breathe. And without it she knew she would be lost.

"Zack," she moaned his name as he held her close. Something about the sound alerted him, warned him that there was something making her anxious.

He kissed her, making certain that when their lips met she would be reassured of his unyielding love. Her soft lips and sweet breath mingled with his own made his heart soar with happiness.

She stepped out of his arms, but not before he saw the tears in her eyes. Ari was upset over something, but then, he guessed, it could be pre-wedding jitters. Every bride has them, he'd been told.

"Come on in, Zack. Food's ready, and I hope you're hungry."

"Starved, honey, I haven't eaten all day. Had a soft drink and some chips, but that doesn't count that as a meal."

"I should say not."

She led him into her kitchen. He was pleased to see the small table she had opened up so they would be comfortable.

"I figured we could eat in here because I have all those printer's sample books and brochures spread all over the living room. You don't mind?" she asked.

"Are you kidding, I've already told you how much I love your house. The table looks great, red checked table cloth, candles in wine bottles...I take it we're eating Italian tonight."

Ariadne smiled, "That we are, signor," and she waved him to a seat in front of the table.

"One moment." He rushed out to his car and returned with a large brown paper bag. With a wide grin on his face he reached inside to place two bottles of wine on her kitchen counter.

"They have both been chilled, one of each, white or red. Don't say I was a Boy Scout for nothing! Be prepared, always, I say!"

The cozy kitchen welcomed him. The piquant odor of tomato sauce redolent of enticing herbs and garlic made his mouth water and he felt his stomach rumble in anticipation.

The cabinets were made of a light birch wood. There was a white electric stove with a light gray ceramic top. The kitchen counter was granite that complemented the stove.

Ariadne retrieved two wineglasses from her cabinet and they sat down to their meal. Zachary poured the wine.

"Here's to us, honey," he raised his glass to her. "To my future wife, whom I love with all my heart."

He leaned over to kiss her and saw a troubled look flash over her face.

"What's wrong, Ari?"

"Nothing, I'm fine," she answered quickly.

She served the food. Zachary pronounced it, "Excellent, girl. You can cook for me anytime."

"As long as you don't mind helping to clean up," she said.

They chatted about their wedding plans and Zachary told her about Henry Kim's reaction when he asked him to serve as his best man.

'I'd be honored,' he said, Ari. Told me how much he thought of you and how lucky I was. Told him I knew that, and now that your brother's situation had improved, there was no constraints to bother us. Clear sailing ahead."

He reached for another roll, somewhat surprised that Ariadne made no comment. Again he was struck by the sensation that some bad hung in the air, he thought, but decided to let the moment pass, for now.

Ariadne looked up from her plate. She had not eaten very much, Zachary noticed.

"Would you like your dessert now or later?" she asked.

"The meal was very good, Ari, and that second roll I had really finished me...for now, that is." He smiled at her, hoping to lighten her mood.

"Why don't you go on into the living room and I'll stack up the dishes in the dishwasher," he offered.

"Well, all right. Seems as if you do know your way around a kitchen."

Her forced lightheartedness did not fool him, however. Something was bothering her and it was up to him to find out what it was. He'd seen too many troubled patients not to recognize the symptoms of distress. And Ari exhibited some of them. She seemed somewhat distant and preoccupied, showed a forced levity as if putting on a 'good' face. And she appeared to be forcing a semblance of happiness about the wedding. Lately she acted as if she was keeping him at arm's length.

He quickly arranged the rinsed off dishes and silverware in the dishwasher, rinsed the wineglasses and set them on a towel to dry on the counter. He found a plastic container for the left over spaghetti dish and placed it in the refrigerator. Then he joined Ariadne in the living room.

She gave him what he thought was a brave smile. "All cleaned up?"

"All systems are go, my dear. What's the next item on the agenda?" He pushed one of the heavy sample books to the floor and sat on the sofa beside her. He placed his arm around her shoulder and drew her close, kissing her on her cheek.

Her face flushed. She blurted out, "I can't marry you, Zack. I want to so much, because I do love you, but I can't marry you."

He leaned back, stared at her in disbelief.

"Girl, what on earth are you talking about? What kind of nonsense is this?"

"I...I...I'm not what you think. I'm not perfect."

His eyes widened as he continued to stare at her.

"Well, damn, who is?"

"This is so hard for me. But, Zack, you deserve the best and...and I'm not it!" she cried, her eyes swimming with tears.

"What on earth are you talking about? Honey, you know how much I love you. My life won't be worth a damn if you don't love me!"

"Zack," she interrupted, "maybe you won't want me..."

"Not want you! Why?"

Almost in a whisper she answered him, "I was sexually assaulted my first year of law school. I was twenty-three."

The tears flooded her eyes, streamed down her cheeks. Wordlessly, he drew her close while her hiccoughing sobs shook her slender body.

"No...nobody knows but you. Never told my family, not even my mother."

"God, my poor baby," he whispered. "It's going to be all right. I'm here and I'm always going to be right here by your side."

His mind raced, knowing that his next words and actions were vitally important if he wanted to have a future with the woman he loved. Shocked by her revelation, nonetheless realizing how much she had suffered and the courage she had summoned to reveal the truth made him love her more.

He continued to hold her in his arms as her crying subsided. Then she told him about it.

"There had been one of those three-day snowstorms that Boston is famous for, and I was so happy to leave my apartment. Finally we had a beautiful sunny day and I was anxious to get to the law library. I had a paper due on Torts…you know, 'a private or civil wrong resulting from an illegal action'…."

"Did you know the guy?"

"No, I didn't."

Zachary held her even closer, gently titled her quivering chin up to his face. He sensed the great tension she was feeling, so he kissed her tenderly, then the moment engulfed them and they clung to each other.

In a quiet, controlled voice, Ariadne told Zachary the rest of her ordeal.

"I couldn't tell my mother. She had her own sorry experience with Ray's father…but she was strong enough to put it in her past and make a decent life for herself and her children."

She looked at Zachary, then seeking his reaction to her shocking news, the caring love she saw in his eyes enabled her to continue.

"I knew I had to follow her example. I was determined not to let that…" her voice cracked, "that creep to mess up my life…to keep me from getting my law degree."

"What did you do?" he asked gently.

"A couple of girls found me…took me."

"And," Zachary prompted.

"They wanted to call the police, but I begged them not to. The doctor treated me for hypothermia. I had cuts and bruises because I had struggled so with my assailant."

"Did you ever notify the police?"

"No, and I begged the doctor not to make a report to the school authorities. But she said she was required to do so. However, she agreed not to indicate that the assault was sexual in nature. I was lucky, Zack, that she was a female physician and understood."

Ariadne tried to focus on Zachary's face, but hot tears seemed to impair her sight. She wiped her eyes, anxious to assess his response.

"I didn't want to tell you all of this, but I wanted you to know, and if you don't want to m…m…marry…" she stuttered.

He pulled her into his arms.

"Girl, hush!" he demanded, his voice thick with emotion.

He felt her soft sigh brush across his cheek as he gathered her close. He felt sexual passions flood his body, but he tempered it with logic. Now was not the time. It was time for affirmation. His voice was soft but firm when he spoke.

"Ari, let me tell you this. I've loved you for a long time, but never more than I do right now. And I know deep in my heart and soul that when tomorrow comes, I will love you more than I do today."

She clung to him as his reassurances penetrated her mind.

"My sweet one, the past events are just that, past…gone…not to return. Ari, I love you and I want you to be my wife."

He wanted her to feel the warmth of his body next to hers, a protective body that would shield her from every harm.

He kissed her gently, her dark eyes filled with tears, her damp hot cheeks, and finally her lovely mouth. Soft moans mingled in harmony from each of them as their tongues explored their mouths.

"Ari, I love you," he whispered into her neck after tearing his lips from hers.

"I know, Zack. I love you." She placed her hands on each side of his face, pulled it toward her own.

"But I'm no longer a virgin," she whispered hoarsely.

"You still are to me! You did not willingly give your virginity away, it was stolen, taken from you. Case closed, do you hear me?"

This time their kiss was gentle and sweet, with the promise of unyielding love.

Quietly, still holding her so close that she could hear his heart beat with a strong, steady rhythm, he whispered, "I promise you a life of happiness, and by God," his voice trembled with emotion, "I will guard you from any harm with my own life because, Ari, you are my life! Remember that, always."

Later that night, as she lay in her bed, she thought about her revelation and Zack's reaction. She wondered what had compelled her to 'test' Zack, if that was what she was doing, by telling him about her 'lost' virginity. In this day of 'women's lib' and sexual freedom, wasn't it archaic for her to be putting so much importance on an incident that occurred so many years ago? But why had she revealed the sordid event to the man she loved? She had had other liaisons before meeting Zack, even came close to believing she had found love once, but somehow there was something that kept her from making a commitment. Most of the guys had been wonderful young men whom she had dated through the years, but what it finally came down to was trust.

She trusted Zack. His stalwart support of her and her family, his professional skill in helping Ray. Somehow he was able to ease her mind, and the 'all's well' feeling that she got from him confirmed that belief. She could trust Zack with her life, her future. She knew that he put her first, and that by loving her he made her a better person.

She sighed deeply, snuggled deep under the bed covers. She was a very lucky girl, she thought, as she drifted off to sleep.

Chapter Twenty-One

The Marriott hotel proved to be an ideal place for Ariadne and her mother, being in the heart of Manhattan.

Ariadne had taken the Amtrak train from Boston, picked up her mother by taxi and now, aboard the train, the two women settled comfortably for the brief ride into the Big Apple.

Seated by the window, Ariadne watched as the train sped by the scenic shoreline of Long Island. Her thoughts turn to Zack. She recalled something she had heard somewhere long ago, that one believes one is loved because one's lover acts in loving ways. It takes more than mere words, and Zack's loving actions on her behalf proved that. She made a decision to enjoy the weekend with her mother. She realized how lucky she was to have such a strong role model, and the love of a real man. She was fortunate, and she knew it.

Her mother was handsomely dressed for the ride in a navy blue knit pants suit with a sparkling white silk blouse. Her hair had been freshly set and her crisp, gray curls gave her a jaunty appearance. Gold studs in her ears, as well as a gold choker only added to her well put together look. Her mother's accessories included a dark brown leather handbag and slender brown flat pumps with a squared toe. Ariadne was extremely proud of her mother.

"Momma, you sure do look good. Look at you! Dressed to the nines! And here I am in my gray wool slacks and this," she pointed to her dark red wool blazer that she was wearing. "Don't know how old this old jacket is…"

"That's all right, honey." Her mother patted her arm. "We'll take care of everything when we get to the city. Anyway, you always look good to me, no matter what you wear. And I know Zachary agrees with me." She smiled at her only daughter. "You know how proud I am of you and the way you and Zack helped your brother with his trials and tribulations. Well," her eyes shone with brief tears, "there's nothing I won't do to make sure you're happy."

"I know, Momma."

As soon as they got to their hotel room they decided to check on the feasibility of a matinee. The concierge was able to obtain tickets the The Lion King for that evening and they agreed that it made perfect sense to watch the Macy's Thanksgiving Day Parade on television in their room, then go to dinner later. Friday and Saturday were for shopping, and Sunday would be their travel day back to New Haven. She planned to return home on Monday and go in to her office on Tuesday.

At the bridal shop on Fifth Avenue, Ariadne found her wedding gown. She had tried on several, none of which she liked, when the sales clerk, a tiny, smartly dressed Jewish woman, returned to the dressing room with one more plastic sheathed gown over her arm.

"I know you're tired, darling," she said in a Eastern European accent, "but please, just one more. You'll see, this is the perfect gown for you. It was made for you."

"I don't know," Ariadne protested.

"Please, darling, just for me?" the sales clerk begged.

Still standing in her undergarments in front of a three-way mirror, Ariadne sighed, stepped up on the dressing platform.

"Might as well, babe, you're still undressed an' all," her mother said as she helped the clerk unwrap the gown from its plastic covering.

Ariadne raised her arms as the two women approached her with the wedding dress. Her arms were slipped into the sleeves and the back was zipped closed. Slowly, Ariadned turned to face the mirror.

She gasped. The wise, experienced sales clerk was right. The gown was perfect.

Mercita's eyes misted with unshed tears of pride when she saw her daughter standing tall and serene in the elegant wedding dress. Suddenly, without warning, her thoughts turned back to the simple white sleeveless dress with the short bolero jacket she had planned to wear when she married Win. She couldn't help but wonder what that future might have been. But looking at her beautiful daughter, she thought, You did just fine, Mercita, girl! Gram said you would.

Chapter Twenty-Two

Returning to the hotel, Ariadne remarked to her mother that she still wanted to find a wedding memento for Zachary.

"Let's drop your gown off at the hotel and then go out again to see what we can find," Mercita said. "What were you thinking of getting for him?"

"A suitable watch. Have it engraved, I think. Henry Kim, his best man, says he'll give it to him just before the ceremony."

"That will be nice. I'm glad you two decided on New Year's Eve to get married."

Ariadne thanked the bellman who held the room door open for them. He placed her bulky wedding gown on a clothes rack, gestured to a nearby bellhop to take it to her room. In the elevator on their way to their room on the tenth floor, Ariadne responded to her mother's comment.

"Both Zack and I figured that after the troubles of the past year, we were making a new life for ourselves and the New Year would be perfect."

"Last year was a doozy one for all of us, that's for sure," her mother agreed, shaking her head at the memory of the past year.

Ariadne could not help but wonder how her mother would have reacted had she known of her problem that had occurred ten years ago. Deep in her heart, however, she was glad that she'd spared the ugly episode from her. It was bad enough that Ariadne and God knew about it, she thought, and now, the man she loved. He'd said he'd stand by her.

She tipped the bellhop, and after freshening up, they returned to the lobby.

"Taxi, ladies?" the doorman asked when they went outside.

He hailed down the next yellow cab that appeared and helped them to get in the cab. Ariadne gave the driver their destination. He said he was familiar with the place, saying over his shoulder, "Find anythin' ya want, good pawn shop."

The cab driver wished them luck when he dropped them off in front of a tiny shop tucked away in the first floor of an old brick building. There was heavy iron grille work over the front door and windows. To Ariadne it seemed impenetrable, but Mercita spotted the entrance bell and when she pressed it, they heard a vibrant peal from inside. Within seconds an elderly salesman dressed in gray slacks with a black smock opened the door.

"Good afternoon, ladies. Please come in."

He proceeded to relock the door, a gesture that disturbed Ariadne, but she thought probably a wise precaution. She noticed the elderly man was wearing a yarmulke, a skullcap worn by Orthodox Jewish men, that made her relax a bit. She had grown up near a synagogue and had seen the familiar headpiece many times before, especially on the Sabbath.

The shop was filled with all kinds of jewelry hanging from every available wall space. The glassed-in jewel cases contained shelves of rings, bracelets, earrings, and even in the dimly lit small room every space seemed to shine, sparkle with magnificent grandeur.

Ariadne took a deep breath as she followed the pawnbroker who shuffled to a position behind the counter.

"How may I help you, Miss?"

Taking a second deep breath, she explained her mission.

"I…I…I'm getting married."

"Mazel tov, congratulations!"

"Thank you. I'm, well, a friend told me I could find what I wanted here in your shop for…for short money."

She raised her eyebrows in question marks.

"Depends."

"On what?"

"On what you want and how much you want to spend."

"It's to be my wedding memento to my husband-to-be," she explained.

"I have what you want," the salesman said. "Take a look."

He reached deep inside a small cabinet, almost like a safe, to bring out a black box with gold margins on its top lid. He placed the box on top of the counter and opened it.

"A finer man's Swiss made watch you'll never see, Miss. New, this watch would cost you thirty-two hundred dollars. It's a steal at that price, believe me."

Ariadne recognized the watch as very valuable. It was white gold and steel, with the perpetual date justified that she wanted. It had a sapphire crystal, a polished bezel with a jubilee bracelet.

"It's very nice. Do you have others you can show me?"

"Yes, many others, but this one is the best."

Mercita had wandered round the tiny shop looking at other jewelry. Ariadne asked her mother to look over the selection of watches displayed.

"Momma, what do you think?"

"It's your choice, my dear, but I do like the one with the sapphire crystal."

The salesman nodded his head.

"See, the Momma knows best," he smiled at Ariadne.

"Engraving? Do you do that?" she asked.

He shook his head. "No, not here. I'm sorry."

"Oh, Ariadne, we can find someone back home in Boston."

"You are from Boston?" the salesman interrupted, eyebrows raised.

"Yes, sir, we are."

"My cousin, Jacob, has a jewelry store on Washington Street. I'll give you the address. He does engraving."

Ariadne's mother returned to her browsing while her daughter concluded her purchase. She turned to leave the pawn shop and went over to where her mother stood, looking over a case of pocket watches.

"I'm ready to leave now, Momma."

"Look, honey," her mother pointed out, "at all these pocket watches. You know your brother never got over losing his grandfather's retirement watch."

"Are you thinking of buying one to replace the one he lost?"

"Somehow, my child, I believe he took it with him to camp. One of the campers may have taken it. I think Ray took it to impress those New York City boys."

"Could be, and he didn't want you to know."

"You know how kids are. But he was so devastated after he couldn't find it...a big part of his heritage. He never quite got over losing that watch."

"So," the salesman said, "would you like to see a pocket watch? We have some fine Waltham watches."

"I think the missing watch was a Waltham," Mercita said to the man. "The one my son lost was rather old. It was his grandfather's watch given to him when he retired from the Navy."

Ariadne saw the look of amazement that crossed over the shopkeeper's face and he clasped his wrinkled bony hands together loudly.

"Madam," he said slowly, "I have it!"

"Have what?"

"Madam," he bowed low, "I have the grandfather's watch! One moment, please."

The two women watched, openmouthed, staring at each other as the man disappeared behind a pair of black curtains in the back of the room. They were still swaying as he hurried back to place a gold pocket watch on the counter.

"I believe this is what you're looking for." Slowly and deliberately he opened the back cover of the timepiece to read the inscription aloud.

Prescott G. Hatcher, Admiral, USN, for fifty years of service.

"Oh my God!" Mercita's face paled with disbelief at the unanticipated discovery.

"Oh my God," she repeated as she reached for the last thing her son's father had given her.

"It's been here waiting for you all these years," the old man said softly.

Chapter Twenty-Three

As they settled in their seats on the train, Ariadne turned to face her mother.

"I can't wait to see Ray's face, Momma, when you give him the watch. You're going back with me, right?"

"I believe I might as well, Ariadne. I can't believe I really have the watch, can't wait to give it to him. What are the chances that we would walk into a pawnshop in New York and find the watch that's been missing all these years? I'd say a million to one, wouldn't you?"

"At least," Ariadne agreed.

"He was such a lovely old man, the pawnbroker," her mother said, thinking back to their discovery.

"He certainly was. I'm glad we got the slender gold bracelets for each of Ray's girls. They are so excited about being my junior bridesmaids."

"I know."

"And you found a beautiful Rolex for Zack." Ariadne's mother stretched her legs out to reach the footrest in front of her. She sighed deeply, feeling more comfortable with her feet elevated. She turned to her daughter as the train roared back to New Haven, smiled and patted her hand gently.

"Like the lady says in the song, honey, 'everything's coming up roses'."

Ariadne wondered if time could change her past. Even if she saw her attacker after all these years, her circumstance would not change. She never reported the rape so there was no police record.

She made her decision. She would go forward with her life, not let some unknown assailant steal it from her. Enough already! But there was one last thing she had to do.

Her mother's thoughts apparently were still on the exciting afternoon they'd shared with the pawnbroker because she asked her daughter, "What was it that old man said, something about a Black teenager who brought the watch in to pawn for fifty dollars, but that he couldn't sell it because of the inscription. Nobody wanted a watch already engraved."

"Right. So he decided not to display it, just put it aside."

Her mother patted her hand again.

"Honey, we're a lucky family."

"Yes, Momma, we are."

"You know why, don't you? It's because we have each other, we're a real family, that's why," Mercita said thoughtfully. "It's what I always wanted…a real, loving family."

Ariadne knew it was something she had to do. She would have no peace of mind until she did so. She had to know the truth of that horrible assault. She went to the school's infirmary.

"I was a first year law student when I was attacked and came here for treatment," Ariadne explained to the clerk at the infirmary desk. "My name is Ariadne Cooper. Would have been about ten years ago."

"Records are only kept here for two years," the clerk said.

Ariadne spotted the nametag pinned to the young woman's left breast. She used it, hoping for cooperation.

"I understand, Ms. Hamlin, so where can I find older records?"

"The older records are available at a storage facility at the medical library, and that is in Worcester. Let me give you the address."

She wrote something down on a memo pad, tore it off, handed it to Ariadne.

"Here's the address and the hours that they're open. Telephone number, too."

Ariadne thanked her, then called Sara. "Sara, I'm on my way out of town. As I recall, I have a three o'clock appointment with Mr. and Mrs. Morton. Right?"

When Sara said she was correct, Ariadne said she would be back in the office before three.

She drove on the Massachusetts Turnpike to Worcester and within an hour found herself looking for the Worcester exit that would take her to the medical library.

As she neared the location, her anxiety increased. Her sweaty palms gripped the steering wheel, her face flushed as she recalled that eventful morning ten years ago. She had to know as much as she could about that horrid experience before she could go on with her life. She had always hated the word 'closure' that so many people used these days to describe the end of an unsavory experience. For herself she knew 'closure' was not what she wanted. She wanted to be able to live with the experience, put it in its proper prospective. Not let it govern her life.

Because of the passage of the Patient's Bill of Rights she knew she was assured of timely access to her records and information.

Following the directions she had been given, she found the facility. It was a granite building with an entrance in the Greek style. She was able to park her car in a small parking lot in back of the two-story building. Located near Holy Cross College, she remembered that Supreme Court Justice Clarence Thomas had received his undergraduate degree there.

She entered into a small lobby and noticed a directory beside a marble staircase that led to the second floor. When she looked over the directory she found that the year she was researching could be found in Room 151, right on the first floor. Her footsteps echoed on the stone floors as she walked to Room 151 at the end of the corridor. She made her inquiry to the middle-aged woman who directed her to an alcove.

"You'll have privacy here, Miss," she said. "I'll bring the record you're looking for to you."

"Thank you."

She had been required to present her personal identification to the woman, was in the process of returning her cards back into her wallet when the woman returned with a slim manila folder.

"There are four pages here. You may read them but you may not keep them. When you have finished, ring the bell," she pointed to a signal bell attached to the desk, "and I will return for the folder. Please sign here and you must sign again when I come back. Any questions?"

"No, ma'am. Thank you. I understand."

With trembling fingers, Ariadne slowly opened the folder. She saw that her name and a file number were on the file tab. There it was, her name, Ariadne Cooper, her date of birth, address and social security number. Below her vital statistics was a notation labeled History. Ariadne read the page slowly, bringing the moment back to her conscious mind.

She read:

History: A twenty-three-year old Black female graduate student presents with a history of sexual assault. Was discovered at eleven a.m. this morning, semi-conscious, lying in deep snow by fellow students. Was able to indicate to them that she was a law student, requested to be brought to student infirmary.

Physical Exam: Vital signs temp 97 degrees, pulse 88, resp. 20, bp 128/80. P.E. reveals extremities pale, cold to touch, but no evidence of frostbite. Victim severely distraught, disheveled in appearance. Clothing in disarray, rescuers state victim's slacks had been pulled down to victim's feet. Undergarments missing. Pelvic exam reveal lacerations, abrasions along inner thighs, dark bruises on outer labia. Rape kit used, stains collected, possibly ejaculate. Internal exam reveal no evidence of penetration, hymen intact.

Treatment: Treated for hypothermia, warm fluids forced, pain medication given, advised to use OTC med for pain as needed. Warm shower given, observed for three hours. Victim requested that neither her family or police be notified of incident. Released at three-thirty accompanied by female classmate who brought fresh clothing. Returned to apartment by taxi. Advised to seek counseling. Return to clinic if necessary.

The signature at the bottom of the page was signed Rose Patridge,

M.D. At the sight of the name, Ariadne recalled how kind and solicitously the young physician had treated her. Funny, she'd blocked out so much of that information. Now she felt as if she faced her demon and come out on the other side.

As she drove back to her office, to her the sky seemed bluer, a cloudless clear sky that mirrored her joyous feeling. She was free, the weight of the past ten years that had encumbered her had been erased by those six words. Her life was her own again. Maybe the assault did not matter to Zachary. She believed him when he said, "Honey, it's who you are and what you mean to me that matters." But it did matter…to her. Now she could stop looking for happiness. She could create happiness with the man she loved. She had been attacked, but not violated, not sexually possessed. She felt more alive than ever before in her life.

Chapter Twenty-Four

Ray had gone to his sister's house to see how they had enjoyed the weekend.

"From the happy looks on your faces, I gather you two had a good holiday weekend?"

They were sitting in Ariadne's living room living, enjoying coffee and post-Thanksgiving holiday fruitcake. Ray had left his daughters in the care of Mrs. Francis, his housekeeper.

"Did you spend your time shopping and running around?" he asked.

His mother answered cheerfully, "We did more than that."

"I got my wedding dress," Ariadne said. "One of our main reasons for going to New York. I'm really happy about it." She got up from her chair across from the sofa where her mother and brother were sitting to offer Ray more coffee.

"Do you want more coffee, Ray? How 'bout you, Momma?"

Ray held up his cup. "Thanks, Sis. You made the fruitcake, didn't you, Ma?"

"Sure did. Soaked the fruit in rum for almost two months, so don't eat too much, you'll be tipsy when you leave."

She smiled at her eldest child. She loved him very much and despite her attempt to be all that she could to him, life had not been kind to him and she regretted that. His stepfather, Alonzo Cooper, whom she had married when her son was six, had been a good father, the only one Ray knew. She'd read once, however, that the first six years of a child's life are the most formative. Could it be, she wondered, that those six years without a father had somehow scarred her son? Would the return of the long lost watch bring him a sense of continuity, a link to his biological father and…would Ray view it as important? He'd been devastated when he had lost it.

She had secreted the watch behind the sofa cushion where she sat. Knowing it was there, encouraged her.

"So you found what you wanted for the wedding dress, Ari?" Ray asked.

"Oh, I did! And I know Mrs. Francis is making the girls' dresses, but I got each of them a gold bracelet. Let me get them, I want you to see them."

She walked across the hall to her bedroom, picked up the boxed bracelets from her dresser and was coming back into the living room when she overheard her mother, "Son, I want you to know that I've always been proud of you." Ariadne decided not to intrude, the tone of her mother's voice sounded serious, so she quietly returned to her room.

Ray could tell by the look on his mother's face that she was in a serious frame of mind. He'd seen that look as a kid whenever he'd brought home a less than satisfactory report card or as a teenager whenever he came home past the agreed upon hour.

Despite the fact that he was now an adult, Mercita Cooper was his mother. As always, when unnerved, he reached inside his coat jacket for a cigarette.

Mercita's eyes widened in surprise when she saw him retrieve a packet of gum and pop a square in his mouth.

"You've stopped smoking, Ray?"

"Trying to, Mom. This girl I met at the survivor's group, Kendra, Kendra Hampton, she…she got me to try to stop and I haven't had a cigarette in a week."

"Oh, Ray, I am so proud of you! And this Kendra you speak of, she's a new friend?"

"Met her 'bout a month ago. Like I said, she lost her husband, has a four-year-old son, so…"

"You've something in common."

"Yeah, she's real nice. Plan on bringing her to Sis' wedding, so you can all meet."

"That would be nice."

"I think so. I like her a lot." His voice grew sober. "I'll never forget Letty, but like Zachary said, I had to say goodbye and let her go." He took a deep breath and sighed audibly. "She'll always be there, tucked up in a corner of my heart."

Mercita felt her heart hammering. She reached over to take her son's hand.

"I know what you mean. We've never talked much about your biological father," she plunged right in with her deeply held secret. "I've always kept the love I had for your father deep inside my heart. Not that I didn't love your stepfather, Alonzo. I did, with all my heart. But," her voice softened, "there is something about one's first love that remains in one's heart. I want to tell you that you are a carbon copy of your biological father, except he was white and you are brown. I know that he loved me, but…"

"But not enough to marry you," Ray protested, bitterness evident in his voice.

"Son, you must remember it was a different time, interracial marriages were against the law in almost every state in the country. And to be fair, I never told him about you, especially knowing that he could not take me to his home. His parents objected strenuously, wanted him to marry someone from their social strata. And, besides, I didn't even know you were on the way until he had gone on his tour."

"Must have been hard on you, Mom."

"It was. But, Ray, I've never wanted for a better son than you."

"I'm proud of you, Mom. You never showed any bitterness or…"

"Why should I? I had a wonderful husband who loved me, two beautiful children who love and respect me…"

Mercita reached up and put her arms around Ray in a firm bear hug. She kissed his cheek, whispered in his ear, "I have a surprise for you."

Withdrawing from her embrace, he stared at her.

"What? Where?"

His mother smiled broadly, put a finger to her lips to forestall his questions, called out, "Ariadne, honey, were are you? I'm going to give Ray his surprise!"

"Be right there, Mom" She grinned when she saw the excited looks on their faces. "Was on the phone checking with my office," she explained when she returned to her seat.

"Ray, the reason I decided to talk about your father was because of something your sister and I found in New York. This!"

She pulled the pawn shop box from the cushion in back of her and handed it to her son.

"What is this?" He opened the box slowly. Open-mouthed, he stared at his mother. "Grandfather's watch! Where did you get it? Oh, Momma, I never thought I'd see it again after all these years!"

Ariadne realized the moment was an emotional one for her mother, so she explained.

"One of Zachary's friends knew I wanted to buy something special to give Zack on our wedding day, so when I told him I'd be going to New York with Momma, he told me to try this particular pawn shop."

Turning the watch over and over, Ray said, "You found it in a pawn shop?"

"Yes, we did. And as we were about to leave the shop…I got a beautiful watch for Zack, the pawnbroker mentioned that he had a watch some teenager pawned…"

"All my fault!" Ray broke in. "I wanted to show off, impress those city dudes at camp. I knew none of them had ever seen a watch like this, never mind owning one."

"The pawnbroker did say it was a teenager. He gave him fifty dollars."

"How come the pawnbroker never sold it?" Ray wanted to know.

"Because of the inscription. He figured no one would buy it, and then he figured the value might go up and someone who knew its worth might pick it up. Never thought it would be returned to its rightful owner."

"What did you have to pay to get it back?"

"Fifty dollars."

"I'll give it back to you."

"You don't have to do that," his mother said.

"Oh, but I do. You told me not to take it to camp but I did anyway. So I have to pay, wouldn't feel right if I didn't."

"Ray, now that you have your grandfather's watch back, how do you feel?" his mother wanted to know.

He shook his head as if to clear his mind.

"It means that the legacy handed to me was from someone who came from a military background. Whether that is good or bad is of little consequence. The fact of the matter is I do have a heritage. I'm not flotsam and jetsam, a castaway, a discard. I am proud of who I am and that means that I'm the son of Mr. and Mrs. Alonzo Cooper, the parents who loved me and raised me. The watch is just evidence that another man's genes are a part of me. And the watch makes him real, that's all."

"And you're glad to have it back now?"

"Ma, whenever you lose something, you're always glad to get it returned."

Chapter Twenty-Five

A fleeting snowstorm blew into Boston on the day before Ariadne's wedding, but the wedding day itself dawned crisp, bright and sunny. The venerable old city was covered with a pristine coat of snow.

The wedding was scheduled to take place at noon. At ten-thirty Ariadne's hairdresser arrived to do her hair and makeup. Marcus had just placed the final hairpin in the elegant French twist he had fashioned for her and was putting the pearl studded tiara attached to a short veil on Ariadne's head when her mother came in with a small white package. She stopped short when she saw her daughter.

"Honey, you look beautiful!" She turned to Marcus. "Doesn't she look beautiful, Marcus?"

"She surely does, ma'am. Prettiest bride I've ever seen!"

Mercita walked around her daughter to view her from every side, then suddenly she remembered her reason for coming to her daughter's room.

"Oh my goodness! I'm so excited, almost forgot." She handed the small package to her daughter. "This came by special messenger."

Ariadne took the package wrapped in silver foil paper tied with a white satin bow from her mother, stepped away from her dressing table to sit on her bed. She patted an empty space beside her, indicating to her mother to join her.

"It's from Zack," she said as she untied the bow and tore away the wrapping paper. Slowly she opened the blue velvet box and gasped when she saw a pair of diamond studs nestled in blue velvet.

Tears filled her eyes as she tried to read the note attached.

My dearest, she read aloud, I want you to know that on this day of days I am the luckiest man on earth. I have no words to tell you what's in my heart. You are my joy, my love, and to see you happy makes my heart happy. I no longer have to search for love. I have found it in you, my Ariadne. You are my life's blessing and I want you always at my side. All my love, Zack.

No one said a word when she finished reading the note. Marcus wiped his eyes, reached for the tissue box to offer tissues to both Ariadne and her mother.

"The man knows how to turn a phrase," he muttered. "He could make a stone weep with talk like that."

"You can say that again," Mercita said, wiping her eyes. "Here, honey," she said to her silently weeping daughter, "Let's wipe those tears away. This is a day of joy! Marcus, think you can repair the damage to my daughter's face?"

Marcus smiled at the teary faced bride. "I can and I will."

With brisk motions he cleaned Ariadne's face with lotion, patted the excess moisture away with deft light touches to her face.

"We'll get you fixed up right away, Ari. Don't worry, you'll be beautiful! Have a seat."

"Thanks, Marcus. I'll try my best not to cry anymore." She smiled at him from her seat in front of her dressing table.

"I suppose you're used to weeping brides, eh, Marcus?" she said.

"Oh, I expect tears. It's a touching time in a bride's life. I'm suspicious if I don't see tears. And sometimes that makes me wonder…how come this bride is so cool? Know what I mean?"

"I think I do. It's like having a dream come true, you hardly know how to act."

Gently and carefully, Ray helped Ariadne arrange her wedding train and settle back in the white stretch limousine.

"You've lucked up on a great day for your wedding, Sis," Ray said.

"It's really beautiful," Ariadne said. "Look at the way the snow outlines the dark wood of the trees, and there's a crystal sheen on the snow. Makes everything look like a scene from one of the Grimms' fairy tales."

"I hope with all my heart that you will be happy married to Zack," Ray said as he held his sister's hand. "I know I owe him for helping me come to my senses, face reality so that I can live again. I owe it to both of you."

"You don't owe anyone," Ariadne said. "You only needed some help to get you on track. You had the inner strength to meet the challenge and you did. I'm proud of you, Ray." She kissed his cheek and he squeezed her hand.

"Thanks, Ari, for that vote of confidence. Well, here we are," he said as the driver edged the limo to the curb in front of St. Gregory's. Pots of holiday poinsettias lined the brick steps on either side of the church's heavy wooden doors which had been opened. The wedding coordinator was waiting for Ariadne to arrive.

"You're right on time, honey, and everything is going smoothly. Follow me," and she directed them to a small room just off the vestibule. "Wait in here and I'll come for you when it's time to start. You look lovely," she reassured Ariadne.

The door opened a few minutes later and Ray's daughters came in, led by Mercita Cooper.

Each child's long hair had been braided into a tiara-like crown with tiny pink roses and baby's breath woven through. Their dresses were sheer white with a rose toned taffeta dress beneath. Their excitement was palpable as they circled around Ariadne.

"You're beautiful, Aunt Ari," Robin said.

"So are you, both of you," she kissed each girl on the cheek. "Let's go get married."

✿

Later, Ariadne confessed to Zachary that she remembered very little. She said everything became a blur except for seeing Zachary waiting for her at the altar. He told her what he remembered.

"When I saw you, Ari, coming to me, wearing that gorgeous white satin gown with the pearls, crystals, embroidery, the white jacket trimmed with white fur, you looked like an angel and all I could think of was how much I loved you and how lucky I was to have you as my wife."

"So it wasn't a blur to you, Zack?"

"Not a bit! I was totally aware of everything going on. Believe me, everything!"

They were in the limousine being driven to the airport to start their honeymoon.

"What time is it, Zack?"

He looked at his watch, gave her a big grin. "Want to know what I think of my wedding gift, eh?" he teased.

"No, I just want to know what time it is."

"For your edification, Mrs. Zachary Richards, its eight-thirty, New Year's Eve, and I do love my wedding gift. Never thought I'd own a Rolax. Girl, you're just too much!"

His face sobered as he took her face in his hands. He held her face gently. "I know I spoke the religious vows in the church that bound us together in front of God and man, but what I'm about to tell you, Ari, is this. I vow that with all the love that is in me, that my sole purpose in this life will be to make you happy, leave no stone unturned to give you peace and serenity for the rest of our lives together. And I swear that when each new day dawns, I'll love you more than I did the day before."

Holding her face tenderly, his hands firm but gentle, he lowered his lips to hers.

Her response to him came swiftly as she recognized the sincerity of the gesture.

She was safe in the arms of the man she loved, would always love. The hum of the car's motor soothed her, she felt herself relax as Zachary's soft caress assured her that all was well.

"Zack," she whispered, "I've wanted this night to come for such a long time…to be your wife. I love you."

His answer came without words. There was no need. His kiss sealed his promise to his wife. Her loving response to him confirmed her acceptance.

At that moment the driver announced, "We're at the airport, sir."

"Come on, honey, let's catch that plane to Paris!" Zachary said to Ariadne as he helped her out of the car.

The driver retrieved their luggage from the trunk of the limousine and placed it curbside.

Zachary tipped him. The driver thanked him. "Happy New Year, sir, to you and your wife. And good luck!" he said and gave a quick salute.

"Happy New Year to you," Zachary said as he and Ariadne received their boarding passes and headed toward the proper concourse.

As they went through the automatic opening doors, Zachary said, "Look out world, Dr. and Mrs. Zachary Richards coming through!"

He grinned at Ariadne and she laughed at him.

"Think they're ready for us, Zachary?"

"They better be, because we're on our way! Better believe it!"

Chapter Twenty-Six

Holding tightly to her husband's hand, Ariadne stared out the cab's window as the taxi driver sped them along Paris' busy, illuminated streets to their hotel.

Within minutes the driver stopped the cab in front of their destination, the Hotel Le Meriden Montparnasse.

"Zack, I never dreamed I'd be in Paris! I can't believe it! I feel as if I'm in a fairy tale city."

Her husband smiled at her. "Honey, you don't know how happy it makes me to see you so happy." He kissed her, murmured in her ear, "I want our honeymoon to be special. Something we'll always remember…"

"Oh, we will," she whispered back. "We will."

Realizing that the cabbie had removed their luggage from the trunk of the cab and was waiting to be paid, Zachary got out, paid the driver and helped his wife out of the car.

Within minutes after signing the hotel register, they were shown to their room by a very attentive bellhop.

"You are newlyweds, n'est ce pas, monsieur, madam?"

Zachary nodded. "We are."

"Congratulations, and welcome to Paris!"

He opened the room door with a flourish and began to point out to Zachary the various amenities the room offered.

The room was pleasantly decorated with a balcony which looked out over the city street. He explained the television set nestled in a French provincial armoire, the room's heat controls, and pointed out a welcome basket of fresh fruit, oranges, strawberries, grapes, as well as a bottle of champagne chilling in a silver ice bucket. A pair of champagne flutes had been placed on a nearby tray with cloth napkins. The bed had been turned down, ready for the couple.

Zachary thanked the attendant, who seemed grateful for the tip he gave him in Euro currency.

As soon as they were alone, Zachary held out his arms and Ariadne accepted his warm embrace.

"Honey, I know you're tired, because I feel a bit travel weary myself, what with the busy day we've had and the time change and all…"

"I'm bushed," she admitted as she slipped out of her shoes and kicked them aside.

"Ordinarily it would be about three in the morning back home and we'd be sleeping."

"Someone told me once that the best way to get over jet lag is to go right to bed and get some sleep. They said you get over it quicker that way," she said, dropping her jacket on the bed giving him a seductive smile.

He knew exactly what she meant. They were going to bed, but not to sleep. "Makes a lot of sense, Ari."

"I think I'll take a quick shower."

"Ok. I'll unpack my bag, then I'll shower."

Zachary placed Ariadne's bag on the luggage stand and watched as she retrieved toilet articles and nightwear from her suitcase. He could hardly wait to join her in bed, make love to her. He'd wanted to for so long, but he knew, considering her past history, he had to make this experience perfect...for her.

As Ariadne luxuriated under the warm shower, she realized just how considerate Zahary was toward her. Not many men would be so tolerant. She vowed to herself that she would welcome his lovemaking. She had married an unusual man and she knew it.

She returned to their room, bringing with her an aura of sensuality. Her delicate fragrance and the soft pearl-like nightgown and robe she wore added to her breathtaking beauty, Zack thought.

"Wow!" He brushed her lips with a quick kiss and hurried to take his own shower. "Be right back, honey."

And he was, within five minutes. To his great disappointment, his bride was sound asleep. He looked down at her curled up in a fetal position. He watched her soft breath flutter the sheet around her lovely face. As he watched her, his whole body flooded with a mounting, surging tide with love for her. He wanted her, needed her, but he could not disturb her. He could wait. She had been through so much, he thought, I can wait and make our special moment all that we want it to be.

Gently, he eased the bedcover back, slipped into the bed beside her, gathered her close to him. She murmured softly, "Zack..."

"It's ok, baby, it's ok."

He kissed her tenderly on her forehead as she nestled into his arms. She did not wake up. His lips were still on her forehead when jet lag overcame him and he, too, fell asleep.

Her eyes filled with tears when she felt his hand gently stroking her face, his fingers moving tenderly, lovingly along her cheeks and chin. Reacting to this stimulus, she moved closer to him to feel the warmth of his body, to feel so wonderfully safe in his arms. Then he kissed her, nearly taking her breath away. Responding, she curled her arms around his neck, nuzzled into him, his beard scraped lightly against her skin, deepening her awareness of his masculinity. His kisses became more urgent, flaming her body as his lips caressed and savored her with such intimacy she veered toward a threshold of unbelievable ecstasy. She could hardly bear it, she had waited so long, had been so desperate for him to make love to her. There had been those tormenting problems, so many unsought impediments in her past that had kept her from the happiness she sought with the man she loved.

"Zack, Zack," she whispered, "love me, please, love me."

Suddenly her eyes flew open. Where was she? Then she remembered. She lay snug up against Zack's strong body, her arms were around his neck, he had fallen asleep.

Omigod, she had been asleep when he had come to bed after his shower. He had not disturbed her, now he was asleep, but she had been dreaming about all kinds of erotic moments. Aroused, she wondered, should she wake him?

Almost as if a sixth sense had alerted him, her husband tightened his arms around her.

"Zack?" she questioned softly.

"I'm awake, babe. Right here with you."

"Oh, Zack, honey, I'm so sorry...didn't mean to fall asleep..."

"Not to worry, sweetheart, you're here in my arms, right where I want you to be."

He raised himself on one elbow to look down at her.

"You are so beautiful, and I'm so lucky to be your husband. Ari, I love you so much. You do know that, don't you?"

"Oh, Zack, of course I do! I love you with all my heart."

"No more talk. Let me show you how much I love you, my sweet wife," he said.

Swiftly he peeled her nightgown down from her shoulders. He drew in a hissing breath as the dim light from the Paris full moon filtered in the balcony's French doors, pouring a golden sheen over her bare body.

"God, Ari, you're so lovely."

She pulled him close, his head on her breasts. She could wait no longer to have their bodies touch. He nibbled at first one rose-tipped breast, then the other. Her body's reaction to the exquisite sensation startled her. It seemed charged and eager to respond to her husband's loving caresses.

She raised her hips to allow Zachary to remove her sheer garment, which he tossed to the floor where it lay as a silent, shimmering witness to the perfect moment that Zachary and Ariadne sought.

His lovemaking was delicate and measured, dictated by his desire to allow Ariadne to keep pace with him as he explored and touched with love all the sensitive areas on her body that she never knew existed.

He watched her excitement mount as her head tossed about, seeking relief from the sweet torture she was experiencing. She held on to him as if she were about to fall into a deep abyss. Their bodies inflamed with heat as the tension throbbed wildly to a fever pitch level.

Ariadne met his rhythm with her own and suddenly, when she cried out for relief, the long awaited, searched for moment of fulfillment, came. Zachary pulled her to his heart, his entry swift and sure. They shuddered back to earth, breathless by the sheer magical beauty of the moment.

Zachary kissed her. "Love you, babe," he whispered in her ear as she lay quietly, her breathing slowly returning to its normal cadence. He pulled the covers over their still heated bodies and she moved into his rms. This time they both slept with the golden blessing of the Paris moonlight.

Chapter Twenty-Seven

Two years later Winthrop Hatcher was fifty-five years-old when he retired from the Navy after thirty-five years of service. He was unmarried, in good health, exercised daily. Over the years had saved his money and now that he was free of his responsibility as a lieutenant commander, dreamed of owning his own boat. With his pension, he'd do ok.

As soon as he had received his 'walking papers', as he put it, he returned to Newport, Rhode Island, to see if he could find the boat of his dreams.

There was no family to greet him. Both parents had died. An only child, he previously informed his family lawyer to sell the house. His childhood memories of the place were not that special. He'd spent all of it at a boarding school, then upon graduation from college had joined the Navy. Still, Newport was the only home he knew, so he returned there.

One of his long-time Navy friends teased him when he mentioned that he hoped to find a single-mast sloop that he could restore and perhaps spend his remaining days living on it.

"Oh, man, you're crazy! Haven't you had enough of boats?"

"Nah, it's in my blood, I guess. Never made admiral like my granddad, but I did retire as a lieutenant commander."

"Well, I hope you find what you're looking for."

"Aim to do just that."

He took a room at Newport's Harbor Island Hotel as a temporary residence until he could decide on what he was going to do with the rest of his life.

The hotel, a fairly modern building, was situated in the harbor with water on three sides. It was reached by a causeway which carried traffic from the city to the hotel.

As he drove to the site in a rental car, he smiled to himself. He certainly had an affinity for water, was never at ease unless he was on the water or nearby a body of water. He remembered having heard some scientist say that humans spend the first nine months of their existence surrounded by water while in the mother's womb. Could that be one of the reasons why he felt more comfortable on water than on land?

After settling into his room he went down to the hotel's bar. It was about three-thirty, with only a few patrons. Some at the bar, a young couple in a secluded corner interested only in themselves. Newly married, Winthrop surmised. It was a quiet scene.

"What'll it be, sir?" the bartender asked him.

"Any one of your light beers will do."

"Coming right up."

When the frothy topped glass was set down in front of him, he thanked the bartender and wondered why he hadn't asked for something more potent than a mild beer. Why was he still living so cautiously? The story of his life, he thought. Never step out of line. Tried and true. Never take a chance. Play it safe.

As he sat at the bar and thought about it, that lifestyle was not living at all, just existing. If he was ever going to have a life, he'd better start taking some risks, and soon.

He beckoned to the bartender, pushed the glass of beer toward him. "Take this back and bring me a shot of whiskey."

He sat alone, nursing his drink, when a man of uncertain age took the barstool next to him. He seemed to be a 'regular' at the bar because the bartender called him by name.

"What'll it be, Bill, the usual?"

"Right, Hank, the usual."

Since they were the only persons at the bar, Winthrop nodded at the newcomer. "Win Hatcher," he said.

His new companion smiled, stuck out his hand, which Win shook. "Bill Harris. Glad to know you. New here in town?"

"Could say that. But I was born and raised here, been away for some years. Just came back…"

"Been 'away'?"

"Retired Navy man."

"How 'bout that!" He reached again for Winthrop's hand. "I'm an old 'tar' myself, I'm Bill Harris."

"No kidding! Win Hatcher."

"Right. Newport's full of us old 'duffers'. How long you been out?"

"Just got out ten days ago. Decided to come back, take a look at the hometown, decide what I want to do with the rest of my life. You?"

Bill thanked the bartender for his drink, a dark, robust beer, Winthrop noticed, took a long swallow, wiped the foam from his mouth with the back of his hand before answering.

"I put in a twenty-year hitch, decided to pack it in, me and the missus figured this was as good a place as any to retire. Been here new 'bout ten years. Kids gone, on their own. Spend winters in Florida. Not a bad life. What'll you be doing?"

Bill, Win noted, was of medium height with a lean muscular build. His eyes were a startling blue, with deep crow's feet at the corners. He seemed to Winthrop like a man who could take care of himself and knew who he was and what he wanted he envied him.

"To answer your question, Bill, I'm not sure what I want to do, except that I've been tinkering with the idea of fixing up an old boat…"

"What'd you have in mind?"

"Well, what I have in mind is a sloop, say, maybe a thirty-six footer. Something I could work on. You know…maybe fix up to eventually live on…"

"I've got a friend," Bill interrupted. "Joachim, 'Jack' Alvares. Portuguese friend of mine. Think he's selling his fishing boat. If you'd like, I can take you by his place, have a look, see if it's anything you'd be interested in."

Winthrop felt a kernel of excitement well up inside him. "Sounds good. When can we do that?"

"Anytime. You name it."

He checked his watch. He didn't know why, he wasn't going anywhere except back to his solitary room upstairs in the hotel.

"Sometime tomorrow be ok?" he asked his new friend.

"Sure, old Jack is always up early, from his fishin' days, you know. Always up before sun up, sometimes to get to the fishin' grounds."

"You can call me here at the hotel after you speak with him. If I'm out, please would you leave a message?"

The two parted company soon afterwards and Hatcher went up to his room. His life has been so regimented by his years in the Navy, he found it hard to keep himself occupied during his free time. He'd be glad if he could find an old tub…something he could work on, keep him busy. He envied the retiree he had just met who had a family to turn to. He had no one.

Suddenly bored and restless, he kicked off his loafers and padded into the bathroom. After a quick shower, he put on a pair of sweat pants and a tee shirt, sat down in front of the television, and surfed the channels. He hardly expected to find anything of interest. The usual news channels, several old movies. He even ran across Gary Cooper and Grace Kelly in High Noon. How many years ago was that film made, he thought. There were several channels of children's skits and teenagers shaking every single part of their bodies, showing their belly buttons.

He scanned from the provocative scene to see what else he could find. God, please, something interesting.

He scrolled to a scene that caught his attention. It was a well-lighed, Olympic-sized swimming pool with a group of female swimmers performing a synchronized routine to a catchy popular tune, something about 'making it in New York'. He started to continue changing the channels, but the exciting tune made him return to the swimmers. Then he realized that the women were not teenagers, but older women of color. They looked like young girls frolicking playfully as they swam in formation, sometimes disappearing under the water, the underwater camera catching every precise movement they made. Their well-shaped brown legs were displayed in tight circles, star formations and several other intricate geometric patterns which were enhanced by their musical selections.

Winthrop found himself holding his breath as the team somersaulted in the water to spring into an upright position, their right arms tossed triumphantly into the air as the sequence ended

The camera panned each woman's smiling face as she left the water to stand in formation at the edge of the pool.

Watching them, Winthrop smiled with vicarious pleasure at their exuberance. They were something special. As the camera zoomed in a tight close-up of one woman's face, Winthrop stared at her, sucked in his breath in amazement. It couldn't be! The dark eyes were the same lovely ones he remembered, the same laughing smile was there. Her hair was covered by her swim cap so he couldn't see the long, luxurious hair that had so bewitched him so many years ago. But it had to be Mercita! Oh God, why doesn't the cameraman pan back so he can see her again? God, if it is Mercita, how can I find her?

He called the television station immediately. After many starts and stops, using the station's automatic menu, he finally reached a real, flesh and blood human who informed him that, "The swimming segment was from a feed from a New York affiliate station."

"Let me ask you, sir," Winthrop asked, "is there any way I can buy a copy of that tape?"

"You will have to get in touch with the originating station, sir. I can give you the number, and the person you want to talk with is Mike Conway."

"Thanks very much. You've been a great help," Winthrop said.

The call to Mike Conway in New York yielded even more pertinent information which encouraged Winthrop that he might be successful in his search.

The information he received from the man in New York was that the segment Winthrop was inquiring about had been taped at a pool in Connecticut. New Haven, to be exact.

Mike Conway added, "I think the event took place at a Y or a senior center, but I don't have real knowledge of that. Just that the location was New Haven."

"Thanks for the info," Winthrop said, anxious to follow through on that concrete information.

Immediately after disconnecting from New York, he placed a call to the New Haven Chamber of Commerce. Armed with telephone numbers of the YMCA, YWCA, senior centers, as well as local schools and colleges that had swimming pools, he started dialing.

His face drenched with sweat, his anxiety level threatened to overwhelm him as he remembered Mercita and the love they shared.

He recalled the futile search he had made to find her on his return from sea duty. No one, it seemed, not her supervisor, Mrs. Osterman, the next door neighbor, Mr. Akira, even the police had no knowledge of the whereabouts of Mercita or her father. It was as if the earth had opened up and they had simply disappeared.

The breathtaking sight of someone that looked so much like Mercita made him feel that just perhaps, after thirty-five years, he would find the one woman he'd loved and lost.

As he punched in the first telephone numbers, he vowed to himself this time he would find her...or at least the woman who looked so much like her.

Chapter Twenty-Eight

It had not been easy for Ray to begin a new relationship but Kendra, a young single mother that he had met on day on the beach in Hyannis, was so open, so friendly that he found himself drawn to her. Her four year old son Grady had played happily with his daughters, almost as if they had always known him.

It did not take him long to let her know how he felt.

Kendra made the wedding decision after Ray asked her to marry him.

"I will, Ray, because I do love you and the girls. I want you to be happy, too."

Ray held her close, realizing what a big step he was taking. But Zack had been right, life was for the living, and he had to keep on living. For himself, for the girls, now for Kendra and her son, Grady, the four-year-old who already acted as if Ray was his father.

"We can take the children with us to the Justice of the Peace and get married," he said to Kendra.

"We could…but let's see if we can find someone that will come to the house and perform the ceremony."

Kendra's decision made sense to Ray.

The yellow pages of the telephone book yielded the names of several justices willing to travel to Kendra's home in Ardmore, in the south shore suburbs of Boston.

Kendra's father and her four older brothers worked in cranberry bogs that had been in the family for two generations. As she explained it to Ray, "It's always been a good living for the family. And my dad grows strawberries in early summer, lets people pick their own, so we're always busy here on the farm."

"Kendra, you know you've been a lifesaver for me. I'm so glad that at last I can put my sorry past behind me…get on with living."

"That's what I want you to do, Ray." Kendra's face took on a serious look as she sat with him in the kitchen of the house he had shared with Letty and the girls.

"Have you had any offers for your house?" she asked him, knowing he wanted to sell the place.

His face brightened. "A real estate agent called yesterday, Kendra. He has a pre-qualified buyer who wants to buy. Seems the buyer's from out of town, relocating to a new job here, and is anxious to settle in! And guess what…he's willing to pay more than the asking price if he can move in within the month."

"Great! Ray, that will fit in with our plans perfectly!"

"I'm real excited about it. I'd like to move my stuff, what I want to keep, that is, down to your place during the children's vacation week in February, if that's okay with you."

"Of course. You know, Ray, we have a large barn with some farm equipment stored it in, but I'm sure there's room if you want to put some stuff in there until you decide what you want to do with it."

"Good thing your folks left you with this big house when they moved to their assisted living place."

"I know, I'm lucky. My brothers all have their own homes and families. They like the work with the cranberry bogs and the strawberries, but they are glad I have the house. And they are tickled to pieces to know we're getting married. They think very highly of you, Ray, and that's a lot coming from my brothers, who always worried over 'little sister,' as they still call me."

Ray reached across the table to kiss her.

"You may be 'little sister' to them, hon, but to me you are my lifesaver!"

Ray and Kendra were married in the living room of the farmhouse, with her family and his family as witnesses to the ceremony.

Ray wore a navy blazer with tan slacks, a white shirt. His navy tie reminded Mercita of how much her son resembled his father. She choked back tears as she watched Kendra, dressed in a simple pink sleeveless dress, stand with Ray as the Justice of the Peace performed the ceremony.

Ariadne was delighted that Dawn and Robin were able to wear the same dresses they had worn at her wedding.

Zack served as Ray's best man, and before the ceremony began he said to him, "I'm real proud of you, man, and I know you're going to be very happy."

"I owe a whole lot to you, Zachary, you know that," Ray said solemnly.

"It's in the past, bro. This is a new day, seize it, and God speed." Zachary hugged him impulsively, indicating a deep feeling between the two men.

Kendra's position as principal of the Ardmore Elementary School made the girls' school transfers run smoothly, which pleased Ray. He was so anxious that they be subjected to as little trauma as possible.

Mercita found a moment after her son's wedding to nab her new daughter-in-law as Kendra was checking something with the caterers in the kitchen.

"Can you give me a moment, dear?"

"Of course, Mamacita," the name Kendra had decided she would use to address her new husband's mother. "How about we go to my room?"

she smiled.

Tucking her hand into Kendra's arm, the two women, giggling like two conspirators, raced up the stairs.

"Whew," Mercita puffed. "I'd better get back to my exercise class and my swimming lessons. Not as fit as I thought I was."

Kendra shook her head.

"Oh no, Mamacita, you look fine! Hope I look as good as you do when I grow older. You're a wonderful role model."

They were sitting beside each other on the bed and Mercita kissed Kendra on her cheek. "You're a sweetheart for saying that to me. And that's why I wanted to have this moment with you, two women who love Ray Hatcher."

"I'm glad that we can sit down together. Ray and I have had such a whirlwind courtship, and I understand how awful the past has been for him."

"That's right." Mercita patted Kendra's hand. "You look so lovely, Kendra, in your wedding outfit. It really compliments your reddish-brown hair." She tilted her head to one side, placed her hand on Kendra's chin to turn Kendra's head so she could adequately view the elegant sweep of Kendra's hair.

"I want to tell you how grateful I am that you are in my family. It makes me happy to see my son happy."

"To me, Mamacita, Ray is a wonderful, loving person, and I'm the lucky one."

"Hope you'll always feel that way."

"I will," Kendra said softly. "I promise."

Chapter Tenty-Nine

As soon as Mercita was satisfied that her children had settled down in their lives, she told Ariadne and Zack when she spent an overnight visit with them before returning to her home in Connecticut, "I'm satisfied now that my children are happy and that's all I've ever wanted. So now I can go on and live the rest of my life. That is, whatever the Lord wants me to have."

"Mama, don't talk like that!" Ariadne said. "You're going to live to be a hundred!"

"Don't know 'bout that. It's the quality of life, not the number of years. Tell you one thing right now," she insisted, "when I get to the point when I don't know up from down, put one of those DNR signs on my chest, do not resuscitate, and let me fade away. Now, Zack, you're a witness to this!" She pointed a finger at him to emphasize her wishes.

"Mrs. Cooper," he said, "your wish is my command. It shall be so."

"Thank you, son, and why don't you call me Mamacita like Kendra does. I kinda like that."

"I do, too. Mamacita, it shall be."

Ariadne was delighted that her mother and Zachary had such a loving relationship. From what she had already observed, Ray's new wife, Kendra, and her mother had already begun to share a healthy, bonding relationship.

"So Ray and Kendra decided not to have a honeymoon?" she asked her mother.

"No, they said they are taking the whole family to Florida to do the Disney bit."

"I think that's great," Zachary said.

"I do, too," Mercita said. "Kendra told me the children were so happy. Robin, the oldest, said, 'I can't believe it! If I knew how to faint, I would!' "

They all laughed.

"There's nothing like a child's happiness," Ariadne's mother said. "Nothing."

☼

Kendra's position as principal of an elementary school extended to five o'clock most days, with a myriad of administrative chores, so Ray usually picked the children up after school.

He was pulling into the driveway when a black sedan drove in behind him. He got out of his car and directed the children to go into the house.

"Be sure to wash our hands before your touch your snacks! I'll be right in as soon as I find out what this gentleman wants."

The man approaching him was a white man of medium height with a thin face, a slow, measured walk as he neared Ray.

Ray thought he resembled the television personality that invited children into his neighborhood. He almost expected the man's voice to sound friendly and neighborly. Instead, a harsh sounding, gravelly voice asked, "Are you Ray Hatcher?"

"Yes, I'm Ray Hatcher. What can I do for you?"

Without answering, the man reached into his inside coat pocket and withdrew a white business-sized envelope.

"This is for you," he said, handed the envelope to Ray and returned to his car.

Speechless, Ray looked down at the envelope in his hand. In the upper left hand corner he read, Plymouth County Courthouse, the address, and the words Official Business.

Slowly, he walked back to his car, opened the door, got into the driver's seat.

What did the court want with him? Wasn't the matter of Letty's death settled? Now what? With trembling hands he opened the envelope that bore his name. He read the information slowly. It was summoning him to appear in court in the matter of Stanley Marshall, Senior, and his wife, Gertrude Marshall, grandparents of Robin and Dawn Marshall, seeking permanent custody of said minor children.

Ray slumped in his seat. How can they do this? Stan gave up all parental rights when he and Letty divorced. The grandparents, according to Letty, he remembered, always said they seemed distant. A Christmas card for each child, with perhaps a five dollar bill enclosed. According to Letty, the girls barely knew their father's parents, they'd had so little exposure to them.

Well, if they thought that they were going to take his girls, they were in for a battle!

When Kendra got home that day she found Ray sitting alone in the kitchen. The children were in the family room watching a television show. One look at her husband's face alerted Kendra that something was terribly wrong. When she kissed him, passion was missing from his usual response.

"What's wrong, Ray? What is it?"

"This!" He thrust the dreaded subpoena into her hands. "That's what wrong!" he told her.

From the stricken look she saw on her husband's face, Kendra knew that something horrible threatened their happiness.

She sat down opposite Ray at the kitchen table, snapped on a small light over the table and read the summons. She reached for her husband's hand.

"Ray, I don't believe they can do this."

She tried to sound reassuring, continued by saying, "We can get a lawyer who will help us. I know we can. I've heard of these situations before at my school. We will never lose the girls, I promise you."

"Kendra, I sure hope you're right. I figured the tough days were behind us...now this. With you, Grady and the girls, I feel like we're a family. I just can't give them up to people who are perfect strangers, and I won't! The children's best interests are what's important and as I see it, we've bonded as a family. I can't and I won't! What should we do first, hire a lawyer?" he asked.

"I'd say that's the first thing we have to do. As I recall, I worked with a lawyer handling a problem with a student. I can't remember all the details, but I do recall he was knowledgeable and won the case. I'm sure I have his name in my files. I may even have the lawyer's name here in my address book. Let's see."

Returning to the table with a bottle of water, Ray sat down, uncapped the bottle and took a deep draft, which seemed to calm him.

"I'm real sorry that something like this had to happen..."

"Don't be. Life always has its ups and downs. We'll weather this and any others that come our way. Aha! Here it is!" She held up a business card and read the name, Jerome Wyatt, Attorney-at-law. She handed the card to her husband.

"I'll call first thing tomorrow. Thanks, hon. Knowing I can do something, get the ball rolling, makes me feel better already," he told her. "Only an hour ago I felt like I had been kicked in the head by a mule!"

"Anyone would feel that way, something out of the blue like that."

"I didn't think I'd be able to go to my computer class tonight, but I believe I can now. I'm going to start a file, put together any legal documents, anything that will help win this case."

He then kissed her before he left the kitchen...this time with passion.

Chapter Thirty

Mercita's drive to her home in Connecticut was serene and uneventful. Her car hummed along as if it was glad to be out on the open road. She hummed along to the car radio.

It was a crisp, cold but bright sunny morning, a typical New England winter morning when anyone outside could enjoy deep cleansing breaths of the invigorating air.

From the car radio, Nat 'King' Cole's recording of Unforgettable intruded into her thinking. As she listened, for some reason the face of Winthrop Hatcher flashed into her mind.

My God, she thought, it's been years since I've thought of Win. I wonder what my life would have been like with Win. The road not taken, I guess.

Abruptly, she changed to another station.

Enough of thinking of the past, of what might have been. Never a good idea, she thought.

As soon as she got home, turned up the thermostat, opened the blinds to let the sunshine in, she telephoned Nika, her best friend and swimming partner.

"Hey, sister girl, what's happening?" Nika said.

In response to a question from her friend about her time in Massachusetts, Mercita answered, "We had a real bad time last year with my son losing his wife and all, but everything seems to be straightening out. My son, Ray, has married a lovely girl. She has a four-year-old little boy. Ray's girls think that he is their 'baby doll'. My daughter, Ariadne, is settling down with her husband. Believe they're in the process of buying a house, and they seem happy."

Her friend, Nika, laughed over the phone. "With all these marriages going on in your family, maybe you should be looking for a husband."

Mercita hooted, "Are you crazy? I'm just getting to the place and looking forward to it big time to when I can do what I want, when I want, and to whomever I want to do it with! Got no time to be taking care of a husband! Not me!"

"Oh, Mercita, never close that door. You never know," Nika responded.

"Oh yes I do, too! Child, I've worked hard all my life raising my son with no father, then after I married Alonzo, went back to school, got my degree and was able to help our daughter, Ariadne get her education. You know she's a lawyer..."

"You told me she has her own practice, you said."

"That's right, and her husband is a psychologist with his own clients.

So…me, I'm glad I can sit down, put my feet up and take it easy."

"Not for long, my dear," her friend advised. "Jack Hunter is getting ready to start us out on a new routine."

"He is?" Mercita said, referring to their trainer.

"Yep. Says he thinks we're good enough for the Senior Olympics."

"Get out of town!"

"That's what he says."

"Probably plans on working us to death."

"Guess so," Nika said. "Don't know about you, but I could stand to lose some of these extra pounds I put on over the holidays. It's so hard to get the weight off, 'specially when you get older."

"Tell me about it," Mercita agreed.

Win located the high school that had the distinction of owning an Olympic sized swimming pool. Also, he obtained the schedule for its community use, which indicated that a women's senior group used it on Tuesday and Thursday evenings from seven to eight-thirty for swimming lessons.

He had to make some plans if he wanted to find out if the face he had glimpsed on the television was the face of the girl he had loved so long ago.

The first Tuesday evening, in his rental car, he waited from his position in the parking area where he could observe everything and…everyone who entered or left by way of the school's main admission door. He suspected there were a variety of activities going on that evening because the parking lot began to fill with cars. He observed teenagers and some older people going inside, but he did not see a group of older women enter the building. Was there a special entrance for the pool? Should he drive around the building to check? And if he did see the person who might be Mercita, what would he do? What should he do?

He put the key in the ignition lock and was about to start up the engine when he saw a group of women leaving the building. They were laughing and chatting with each other, Win observed, as if they were young, carefree teenagers.

Frantically searching their faces as they moved toward their cars, Win could not identify anyone that looked like she could be Mercita. Maybe she hadn't shown up for practice that evening. He turned the ignition key again, prepared to leave, but what the hell, he thought, I'm going inside! He turned off the motor, jumped out of the car, raced inside the school. A well-built, athletic looking young Black man was signing a clipboard while speaking with the man at a central desk in the school lobby. Win waited until he had concluded his signing out, then approached him.

"Winthrop Hatcher, sir," he said as he offered his hand.

"I'm Jack Hunter. How may I help you?"

"I've seen your swim team on television. You are the coach, aren't you?" He had decided to be truthful and find the information he needed. He plunged ahead. "I thought I recognized one of your swimmers as someone I knew many years ago. Mercita...?"

"Oh, you mean Mercita Cooper, one of our best swimmers. She's very good."

"Do you know how I can reach her? It's been years..."

"Don't know if I can do that," Jack Hunter said. "But if you give me your card, I'd be happy to give it to her." There was notable caution in his voice and Win respected that.

"I'd appreciate that. Here's my card."

He scribbled his hotel address and phone number on the back of the card before he handed it to Jack.

"Just retired from the Navy and this is where I'm living, for now."

Jack placed the card in his wallet. "I'll see that she gets this."

"Thanks again. I'd really like to contact her."

Jack Hunter watched Win leave the building. Wonder who he is and why does he want to hook up with Mercita? He looks very familiar to me, but I can't place him.

Jack Hunter had once met Mercita's son, Ray, when Ray attended a dress rehearsal of the senior women's routine. There were several other enthusiastic children, grandchildren and assorted relatives at the event, and Jack did not remember them all. In fact, he had forgotten most of them, including Ray, but Hatcher's resemblance to someone he had once seen pricked at his memory.

He placed the card inside his wallet. He'd give it to Mercita when he saw her on Thursday.

Chapter-Thirty-One

Jerome Wyatt, attorney at law, looked a lot like Johnny Cochran, except that he was taller and a few years older.

Kendra and Ray went to his office in the Prudential building in Boston.

"I don't know that we can afford him" Ray said to Kendra as they parked their car in the underground garage.

"We'll never know until we ask," Kendra said. "We have to think positive, that's all."

The lawyer's secretary ushered them into a comfortable conference room. A large oak table with seating for six dominated the room. The walls were covered with citations, honorary degrees awarded the lawyer, as well as a huge wall-sized photograph of the New York skyline, taken at night.

The secretary offered each of them coffee, but both declined.

"Well, if you change your minds it will not be a problem for me, or would you like something else?"

"Water would be fine," Kendra said.

"No problem and Mr. Wyatt will be with you shortly."

"So many changes in our lives," Ray said. "Just when you think everything is going smooth, the other shoe drops."

Kendra patted her husband's hand.

"Honey, we've got each other. We'll get through this, and be stronger for it," she tried to reassure him.

At that moment the lawyer entered the room, followed by his secretary who carried a silver tray with a pitcher of iced water and glasses. She set it in the center of the table.

The lawyer extended his hand to Ray, who stood to shake it.

"Nice to meet you, sir."

"Thanks for meeting with us," Ray responded.

"Mrs. Hatcher?" the lawyer greeted Kendra, who also shook his hand.

"We appreciate any help you can give us," she said.

"Let's see where we are, shall we?"

The lawyer pulled a legal pad toward him, picked up a pen and nodded to Ray.

"My two daughters, Robin and Dawn, are not my biological children," Ray explained. "When I married their mother she had full custody of them. Their father, Stan Marshall, gave up all rights to them."

"As part of his divorce settlement with his wife?" Wyatt wanted to know.

"Correct, but then he started coming around after our marriage. I had legally adopted the girls and he began to try to come to our home, demanding to see the girls who, by the way, scarcely knew him, and finally we were able to get a restraining order."

"Which did little good," Wyatt surmised. "Quite often are not too effective," he added.

"I believe it made things worse," Ray said. "Mr. Wyatt, sir, my daughters do not know these people. Their father was out of their lives very early on. Their lives have already been upset and we're starting over as a real family with my wife, Kendra, and her son. The girls are real happy with the way things are."

The lawyer nodded in agreement. "I quite understand." he said, adding, "In preparation for our initial meeting this morning I did a little research on your late wife's unfortunate accident. I presume you were a prime suspect."

"That's right, sir." Ray's face flushed immediately.

Wyatt took note that Kendra reached for her husband's hand. A really supportive gesture, he thought. Hope I can help them through this crisis.

"I was suspected, but the D.A.'s final decision was that I was not guilty of Letty's death. But you know, sir, I still feel the blame…because, because," he stuttered, "I did bring the gun into our home. It was because of all of the problems we were dealing with Stan Marshall. But…the gun…the gun that bothered her so much, having it in the house, she got so shook up over it, I put it away, safe or so I thought."

"I understand. We'll try to get this all sorted out. Judge Alexander of the Family Court is a fair and understanding woman and always has the best interests of the children in mind. One thing I should tell you, she may make a decision that the grandparents have visitation rights. That is, she may bend in that direction, particularly if she feels the girls are securely bonded with your family."

"They already love my mother, my sister, Ariadne, and her husband. Even took part in my sister's wedding."

"As I said, the judge will listen to all the arguments."

"They have been through enough," Ray persisted. He looked at Kendra, who nodded her head in agreement.

"The court may even insist that a social worker supervise a visit between the children and their grandparents at a designated neutral setting to observe the interactions between the older couple and the girls. Judge Alexander will want to know how the girls react to their grandparents. And you should be prepared to accept visitation rights if the judge makes that decision."

Kendra spoke for the first time. "You know, sir, for the sake of the girls' best interests, we are reluctant to place them in any more traumatic situations. All we want is what will make them happy and well-adjusted. Right now they seem to be making a reasonable adjustment. Both have already made friends in their new school..."

Wyatt gave her a wry smile. "I'm sure it helps having you the principal of the school."

"Well...maybe," Kendra smiled back at him.

"Guess I'll have to tell Ariadne, Zack, and my mother what's been going on," Ray said to his wife as they drove home after the visit to the lawyer. "I know they are going to be upset. I feel so much guilt over the whole situation. They have been so willing to stand by, support me, help me..."

"That's what families do, Ray. They support each other. And your family will still support you, I'm certain of that."

"One thing, Ray," Kendra said as she pressed a light kiss on her husband's cheek. "I do believe this lawyer, Jerome Wyatt, will do his best to help us, don't you? I felt real comfortable talking with him today."

Ray took his right hand off the steering wheel to pull his wife over in a quick hug. Her face glowed with love and confidence.

"That's what I love about you, girl, you are always optimistic, full of hope."

Ray called his mother that night about eight o'clock, but she was not at home. He didn't leave a message on her answering machine because he did not want to worry her. He did manage to reach Ariadne. Her response to his problem was an angry one, as he expected it would be.

"Who are these people? They can't do that! Coming out from nowhere."

"They live somewhere near Worcester, I think, I'm not sure," Ray told her. "I remember Letty saying once that Stan took her out to meet his folks, but that's all."

"You've already seen a lawyer, you say?"

"This morning. And we both, Kendra and I, feel that he is going to be able to help us."

"Who did you see?"

"A lawyer that Kendra knew, Jerome Wyatt."

"He's very good, I hear," Ariadne said. "But you know, Ray, you could have asked me. I have several friends who handle cases..."

"I'm sure you do, Sis, but Kendra and I...well, we decided..."

"Well, if you do need my help..."

"I know I can count on you, and I do appreciate your offer, really I do," Ray said.

"Does Mama know?" Ariadne asked.

"Tried to call her, but she's out…"

"Her swimming class, no doubt."

"That's right, it's Thursday, one of her swim nights. I'll try later."

The swimming session over, Jack Hunter approached Mercita, his clipboard in hand.

☼

"Mercita, can you stop by the office on your way out?" Jack Hunter asked.

"Of course, no problem," she said. Turning to Nika, she said, "I'll meet you at the car."

"Take your time," her friend answered.

Mercita gathered up her duffle bag containing her swimming equipment, her purse and car keys, to follow Jack to the small office he had been allowed to use. It really belonged to one of the part time teachers who agreed to let him use it.

"Yes, Jack, what can I do for you?"

"Mercita, it's not what you can do for me, it's that I hope I haven't done anything to you."

"To me? What are you talking about?"

She noticed the somber look that came over the instructor's face. She sat down quickly. What was it?

"Well, tell me! Explain what you're talking about, Jack."

"Last Tuesday a white man, looked like he could be around fifty, fifty-five, came in asking for you."

"For me? Who was it?"

"He wanted to have your address. Of course I told him that I couldn't give him that information, but if he would give me his card I'd pass it on to you. And if you wished to contact him, that would be your decision. Here's what he gave me."

Mercita read the name on the card. Her eyes widened as she recognized the name. Winthrop Hatcher, LCDR USN(Ret). Below the name, a Newport address had been scratched out and a telephone number for the Newport Harbor Island Hotel had been written.

Silently, she stared at the card, aware, too, that Jack was judging her reaction. She drew in a deep breath, forced herself to exhale slowly. Then in a quiet voice she explained to the obviously curious young man, "Someone I used to know, years ago."

Chapter Thirty-Two

As she walked to her car in the parking lot, Mercita stuffed the card into her purse. Win, Win Hatcher, why did he have to show up in her life now? It had been thirty-five years. Should she let him back into her life? Thirty-five years is practically a lifetime. She'd raised her children. They seemed happy…so far. Now Win?

Nika was standing beside Mercita's car, chatting with Amanda Pierce, one of the other swim team members. The three women said goodbye. Amanda got into her Volvo and drove away. Mercita and Nika followed in Mercita's car.

"So," Nika asked as Mercita negotiated out of the school's drive to the street, "what did Jack want? Is he changing our routine?"

"Oh no, nothing like that. Seems like a friend from California, someone I haven't seen in years, is in town and wants to find me."

Mercita tried to sound nonchalant about the whole thing, but her hands were sweaty on the steering wheel, and although she was trying hard to sound matter-of-fact, she knew Nika would tune into her anxiety no matter how hard she tried not to show it.

Nika remained silent.

The telephone message light was blinking when Mercita walked into her bedroom. She punched the play button, smiled when she heard her son's voice.

"Hi, Mom, just checking in. All is well here. Talk to you later. Bye."

Why hadn't she noticed before how much Ray's voice resembled Win's? She hadn't heard Win's voice in years, but there it was, the same timbre, same cadence, the same warmth. Suddenly she could see Win as she remembered him. Tall, lean, with the broadest shoulders she had ever seen. His blue-green eyes seemed able to see right into her soul. Stunningly attractive in his sparkling white Naval officer's uniform, his quiet manners, his sensitivity in convincing her that he cared for her deeply, that she was the core of his existence.

She remembered the night vividly when he informed her about his parents' reaction when he told them about wanting to marry her.

"None of that matters to me," he insisted. "This is my life, and I want to spend it with you. I want you to be my wife. Merci, you know how much I love you."

A week later their situation became even more traumatic. He told her that he had received orders to ship out.

His face flushed with anxiety. He begged her, "Please, Mercita, marry me! I only have ten days before I must leave the base." He tried to pressure her, his sea-green eyes imploring her to agree.

"I think we should wait until you get back," she told him, mindful of his parents' rejection of her.

"But I want to marry you now! I don't want to wait."

He kissed her then, and despite her resolve, when their lips met, flames of desire flared. A powerful, roaring conflagration that threatened to consume them. Both were acutely aware of the dreaded separation that loomed like an ogre in their future. That night their lives changed forever.

She got up from her seat on the bed and walked into her bathroom. She leaned over the sink and stared at her image in the mirror. She saw a middle-aged, tawny-brown skinned woman with a head of short, crisp gray curls. Her face was smooth and unblemished, but there was a slight softening around her jaw-line, as well as a slight thickening of her body around her waist and hips. She could easily see that she was not the petite, sylph-like young woman Win Hatcher had seen over thirty years ago.

Although many of her friends said she was a very attractive widow, she wondered what Win would see.

Her memory of him was a tall naval officer whom she had loved, whose son she had given birth to and raised.

Ray had suffered so much as a fatherless child until she had married Alonzo, who became the only father the child knew and loved.

She sat down on her bed, picked up the phone receiver and dialed her son's number. His welfare was her priority.

"Ray, honey, how are you? Just now got a chance to return your call."

Chapter Thirty-Three

A few nights later, Ray reached his mother by phone. She was very upset.

"But Ray! They can't do that, can they?" Mercita's horrified exclamation interrupted her son's litany of his recent legal problems with the elder Marshalls.

"Our lawyer says 'yes,' they do have the right to file a petition to get custody of the girls because they are their biological grandparents."

Mercita declared, "I'm coming right up to your house. I'll drive up in the morning."

"Momma, you don't have to do that."

"I know I don't have to, but I want to…to help in any way I can."

"But Ma, there's nothing you can do," Ray insisted in a firm voice. "Right now, anyway. The case won't go to court for maybe several months. The lawyer says the Family Court calendar is full. Anyway, just knowing you're in our corner, Momma, is all you can do for us right now."

His mother sighed heavily.

"I just don't understand people like that. Those little girls, from what you've said before, don't even know those grandparents."

"That's right. That's why it's so hard. It's not like there's a good relationship. Kendra and I feel that we have to deal with this. It's our problem and we will handle it."

"Well, I'm proud of you, son, real proud. You sure have had your ups and downs, but you seem to weather the storms."

"You taught me that, Ma…"

She broke in, "Ray, you've never been anything less than a wonderful son. I…I just wish life had been easier for you.

Unbidden, the thought came to her that the lapse of self-control had been hers. She should not have fallen in love with that Navy man. Bu she had. That golden night produced her son…hers and Win's. She had no regrets in spite of all the hardships she had endured.

She said goodnight to Ray, with his promise to keep in touch. Then she made her second call.

The voice she heard on the other end was the same as she remembered. "Hello, this is Winthrop Hatcher." Listening to the firm, intense voice, Mercita realized she could still be affected by it. Her palms were wet, her face felt unbearably hot, and she was holding her breath.

She took a deep breath before she answered.

"This is Mer…"

"Mercita! Oh God, Mercita, you called! I was so worried you wouldn't call back! Where are you? When can I see you? Oh my God, it's been so long!"

"I know, Win. Thirty-five years." Mercita answered dryly, trying to sound matter-of-fact and trying to calm her nerves at the same time.

"How are you, Win?"

"I'm great, now that I've found you! When I saw your face on the television screen, that's how I found you, when I saw your beautiful, lovely face I couldn't believe my eyes! Why did you leave San Diego? When I got back from sea duty you were gone and I couldn't find you anywhere! None of our friends had seen you. Oh Merci, when can we get to see each other?" The questions tumbled in rapid fire sequence from him.

"Well, to be truthful, Win, I'm not altogether sure that we should...it's been so long."

"I know, Merci, I know." His voice grew more somber, as if reluctant to ask his next question, but he plunged ahead. "Have you had a good life, Mercita?"

His question did not surprise her, even after all these years. It was like him to show concern for her welfare. But now there was a different set of circumstances directing their lives. She was no longer a naïve teenaged Black girl with limited skills. The past years had brought substantial changes in her life. Today she was a self-assured, confident, educated woman, the mother of two wonderful children. She owned her own condo, her own car, and was able to live a comfortable, enjoyable lifestyle on her late husband's survivorship pension he had provided her, plus her own savings. She was, she liked to think, her own woman.

Now suddenly she faced a problem. What, if anything, did she owe Win? How about Ray? What were her obligations to him? Did he have the right to know his father? She was the pivot on whom the future of each man rested. Should she bring them together? Was that her responsibility?

Suddenly it dawned on her that perhaps subconsciously she had made that decision when she picked up the phone to make the call to Win.

His voice broke into her thoughts.

"Mercita, you are going to let me see you, aren't you? Please, just tell me and I will come to you. Connecticut or anywhere! I have to see you! You know I've never forgotten you..."

"You know, Win, thirty-five years is a really long time. A lifetime, really, and I'm not the same person..."

"Nor am I," he interrupted. "Merci, did you get married, have a family?"

She wondered why that particular information was important to him, but she answered, "Yes, Win, I have two wonderful children that I'm very proud of, needless to say. They have brought me much joy."

"You're a fortunate woman. I...I have no family. My parents died some years ago and, well, Mercita, I never married."

"Never?" she asked, incredulously

"Never. Never even got close. There was only one person I wanted in my life. You."

After she hung up the phone, thinking over their conversation, she realized that Win's only living relative could be their son. That became the reason for finally agreeing to meet with his father.

Win had insisted on driving to her home in Connecticut, but Mercita said she would rather meet at a restaurant for lunch. He agreed to that idea. They were to meet at twelve-thirty at an inn that Mercita was familiar with. A well-known restaurant located on Long Island Sound, near Mystic, Connecticut. It was about fifty miles from her home. She planned to arrive at the place a half-hour before Win's expected arrival.

She had awakened that morning with mixed emotions. She wanted to see Winthrop Hatcher, but on the other hand her own life was finally obtaining some measure of equilibrium, except for Ray's custody problem. But both he and Kendra felt they could deal with it. She fretted over her decision to see Win, but they shared a child. Her life would change, that fact was irrefutable. Did she have the stamina to face whatever changes followed as a result of today's meeting?

She went to her closet to get the designer gray wool crepe suit she'd splurged on when she and Ariadne were shopping Thanksgiving weekend in New York.

Designed with a jacket that fitted her waist, minimizing her weight problem, it sported a gently flared skirt ending at her knees. She wore a black and white abstract patterned silk blouse. For jewelry, her diamond stud earrings and her engagement and wedding ring. Before he died, her husband, Alonzo Cooper, had given her a diamond bracelet. He'd said at the time, "Diamonds are your birthstone, honey, and I want you to have as many as I can give you."

As she fastened the clasp, she recalled the moment. She was indeed a lucky woman. She had been cherished by a wonderful man. Would the memories of that relationship sustain her in the present?

She went into her bathroom to check her carefully applied makeup for the millionth time. Peering at her face in the mirror, she chuckled, stop it, girl! Thirty-five years of living is right on your face. There's only so much the most expensive makeup can do. Ok, Win, you asked for it. What you see is what you get!

Then she quickly turned away from the mirror, grabbed her purse and car keys from her dresser, threw her winter coat over her shoulders and headed out the door to meet the first man she had ever loved. On the passenger seat lay an envelope. She sighed, placed her handbag on top of it and slowly backed out of her driveway.

Chapter Thirty-Four

The inn Mercita was heading to was located a mile or so off Route 95. As she drove through several small coastal towns she began to feel relaxed by their calm, tranquil atmosphere. She finally drove into the parking lot of the Griswold Tavern well ahead of her planned meeting with Win.

After finding a parking space very close to the restaurant's front entrance, she considered remaining in her car, perhaps to get a glimpse of Win as he made his arrival. When they had talked on the phone, making plans for their meeting, he had told her, "I'll be driving a rental car, and you?"

"I have a Mercedes," she had responded, and before he could make a comment about her owning an expensive car, "It's not new, but it does well by me."

As she sat in the car, reflecting on the events that had brought her to this point in her life, she thought how silly she was to delay this long awaited moment. Why was she acting so cowardly? Why not go inside, face the future, whatever it was going to be? She had already dealt with her share of difficulties…having a baby alone, raising a child when she, herself, was slightly more than a child.

After Win had left for his sea duty assignment, she had returned to South Carolina to live with her maternal grandmother. Those bleak days and nights were filled with confusion because she did not understand what was happening to her body.

Shaking her head as the past sorrowful memories emerged; Mercita left her car to enter an attractively furnished lounge where she and Win would meet each other before having lunch.

She spotted a comfortable wing chair in front of a fireplace with a bright, crackling fire that added warmth and comfort to the room. A flickering ceramic lighthouse graced the brick mantel, joined by hand carved wooden duck decoys and other waterfowl. A large colorful photograph of an underwater scene was mounted on the wall over the mantel.

Several sofas slip covered with nautical colors of blue and white, deep armchairs situated around the room added to its homelike atmosphere.

Mercita settled into the chair, took deep breaths to try to calm her embattled nerves and looked toward the double doors by which Win would enter.

Trying to return to her usual practical self, Mercita momentarily closed her eyes, listened to the soft music filtering into the room.

Suddenly something alerted her. She opened her eyes and saw him, his eyes scanning the room, much as he had probably searched countless horizons when at sea.

He was still tall, with a military bearing, still slender, but his hair was no longer the golden blond she remembered. Today it was a steel gray crew cut that added to his mature military stance.

Her heart pounded wildly in her chest as if to leap out of her body. Where had her resolve gone? For thirty-five years she had been able to live a creditable, secure life without this man, how could the mere sight of him do this to her?

She didn't trust her emotions as she watched Win glance around the room, his brilliant blue eyes searching.

Watching him, she realized that here was the only man who had led her towards unbelievable paths of ecstasy, who had brought her to such sensational heights of sweet torture her body had vibrated like a finely tuned harp when its taut strings were plucked. The exquisite memories overwhelmed her. With tears in her eyes, she stood up. Then Win saw her. Within two strides, he crossed the room, his arms outstretched, he reached her. She walked into his arms, her legs trembling at every step.

"Merci, Merci," he groaned as he held her close. "At last I've found you."

"How are you, Win?"

"Life has treated you well, Mercita. You are more beautiful than ever," Win said as they moved to sit on the sofa facing the fireplace.

"Thanks, Win. I try to take care of myself, watch my diet, exercise…"

"Thank God!" he interrupted her. "I might never have found you if you hadn't been televised with your swimming team."

For Mercita, somehow the years had rolled away and the man who held her hand so tightly was the same as before. Except for his frost-tinged hair, and instead of Navy whites he was wearing a dark brown blazer with tan slacks. She still felt the same magnetism that had enthralled her a lifetime ago. It was his way of making certain that she knew she was the most important person in his life. But could she ever really be that person? Wasn't it too late, thirty-five years too late? She couldn't return to being nineteen again, and her subsequent life experiences had molded a tough shell around her to help her deal with life's many onslaughts.

She pulled her hand from Win's grasp, asked him, "Are you still in the Navy?"

"Oh no, I'm retired now, Mercita. Just a plain old retired deck-swabber."

She laughed. "You've never swabbed a deck in your life, Winthrop

Hatcher!"

"Once or twice, maybe," he said, reaching for her hand again. "Tell me, Merci, why did you leave San Diego? You knew I was coming back, that I wanted to marry you. When I got back and couldn't find you...I almost went crazy, thought of going AWOL to look for you. Look," he reached into his inside jacket pocket and brought out a slim red lacquered flat box that had been tied with a silk gold cord. "I've carried this around with me for thirty-five years. I always knew that somehow we'd find each other." He handed her the slender box. "Brought this back from Japan."

She slid the cord from the box and opened it. Under slightly yellowed tissue paper lay a gossamer gold silk embroidered scarf as fine and delicate as a butterfly's wing.

"Win, it's beautiful," Mercita said as she fingered the luxurious folds. "It's so delicate!"

"Just like its owner..."

Mercita knew that because of her past involvement with Win, she had to tell him why she'd left California before he returned.

"I...I have something to show you, Win. One moment..."

She opened the eight-by-eleven brown envelope and withdrew a picture of her family. It was Ariadne's and Zachary's wedding photograph. The wedding couple was in the center. Mercita stood next to the bride, Ray and Kendra were positioned next to Zachary, and the little girls and Grady stood in front of their parents.

"I'd like you to meet my family."

He reached for the photograph and looked at it.

"What a handsome fami..." Then his voice choked with emotion. "My God!" when he saw Ray's photo in the group picture his eyes widened with his discovery.

"Mercita! That young man! He's, he's my son...ours, isn't he? My God, I know he is! It's like looking into a mirror! Why didn't you tell me we were going to have a baby? Why?" His voice strained under the emotional upheaval he felt, his blue eyes glistened with unshed tears at what might have been.

"How could I have told you something that I didn't even know about? I didn't know I was pregnant." At that moment he saw tears in her eyes. Impulsively, he pulled her close, as if he never wanted to let her go.

For a brief moment they clung to each other, then Mercita pulled away.

"His name is Ray, and this is his wife, Kendra, and their two daughters and Kendra's son. The bride is my daughter, Ariadne, and her husband, Dr. Zachary Richards, a psychologist."

"I can see that you are very proud of them."

"Indeed, I'm proud of all of them. They're better than I deserve."

"Not so, Mercita," Win interjected. "You deserve the best. Please, won't you tell me about..." he hesitated, "about Ray?" He leaned toward her as if to be certain he would hear every detail about this unexpectedly new person in his life.

For a brief moment Mercita stared at the flickering flames of the fire, wondering what changes her net words would mean to her, to Ray, to her family.

Winthrop waited, his eyes fixed on her face as he yearned to hear about his son, his only living relative.

Finally, after what seemed to Win to be a lifetime, Mercita turned to him. The look she saw on his face revealed the same anxious, uneasy expression she had seen on her son's face many times. Momentarily taken aback, she realized that father and son shared many mannerisms, traits and ideas that she had thought were learned, but at this moment Win's eagerness to learn about his son was very evident in his intensity as his eyes never wavered from Mercita's face. It was as if his whole body was centered on her and what she was about to reveal.

Chapter Thirty-Five

"His name is Ray, Ray Hatcher…"

Win broke in, "You gave him my name?"

"I did not," Mercita responded in a firm voice.

"But, but how?"

"It was my son's decision."

Our son, Win thought, our son, wondering if he'd ever hear Mercita say those words.

She continued to explain the name change.

"Ray's adolescent years were, well, they were hard for him. Really difficult at times."

She saw a remorseful twinge flick across Win's face.

"His stepfather, my husband, Alonzo, was a great father to him, but I think it was when Ray went to summer camp, he came back wanting to know about his biological father. That was when I told him about you, and I gave him the watch…the one you had given to me."

"I remember," Win said quietly. "It was all I had at the time that was of any value, and I wanted you to have it, to know how much I loved you, Mercita."

"My son did ask me first if I had any objections to him changing from Medieros to Hatcher and I told him I had none at all, if it was what he really wanted to do.

His reasoning was simple. Early on he asked me once if he resembled his father. I told him, 'Yes, except that, Ray, your eyes and hair are dark. Otherwise you look very much like your father.'"

"Do you think that's when he decided to change his name?"

"Believe so. Seems he figured out if he looked like you, he had a right to the Hatcher name."

"God knows he has every right to it," Win said solemnly.

"Yes…well, he decided as soon as he reached his eighteenth birthday he would file a petition with the Family Court for the right to change his name. Last name, that is. His stepfather and I offered to help with the lawyer's fees, but he said he 'didn't need our money. He had saved up to do this'."

"Have to admire his determination," Win said.

"That's what the judge said when he asked Ray about his decision. He told the judge that his parents could not marry because of the miscegenation laws that prohibited inter-racial marriages, but that should not keep him from carrying the name of the man who was his biological father. The judge agreed."

Win sat back, shook his head in astonishment. He remained quiet for a moment, and then he impulsively reached for Mercita's hands.

"I know one thing for certain. My son has fortitude and determination. He got that from you, Merci, his mother. If I'd had more backbone, Ray would never have found it necessary to claim the heritage that was rightfully his. I hope somehow that I can make it up to him. When can we meet? I can't wait!"

The wide excitement in Win's eyes and the deep reddening of his face told Mercita how much her news had affected him.

"Please, Mercita! When can I meet him?"

Knowing how much Ray had always yearned for a father, Mercita nonetheless knew what this revelation would mean to him. She had to prepare him, and Win would have to understand and…wait.

"I know how much this means to you; Win, but I just can't drop such a bombshell…"

"I know, you're right, and God knows all I want is to see him, touch him, acknowledge him as my own flesh and blood. Merci, can you imagine what this means to me, finding you and our son?"

Mercita checked her watch. The afternoon traffic would be clogging the roads soon, and she wanted to get home before dark.

"I have to leave, Win. The traffic, you know. But as soon as I get home I will call Ray and let him know…"

"Please, Mercita, please do that. I can't wait to meet him. Anyplace, anytime."

"I know," was her reply. "We'll have to let him decide."

As Mercita lifted the phone from its cradle, she recalled the problem her son was having with the girls' grandparents. She hoped her news would not overburden him, although she had seen Ray rebound from the past events and he seemed to her to be stronger because of, or in spite of, the untoward circumstances. She was pleased that he had been able to get on with his life.

Kendra answered the phone on the first ring.

"Hello, the Hatcher residence."

"Kendra? Mamacita here. How is everything?"

"Oh, Mamacita, we're all fine. How are you?"

"I'm fine, Kendra. Is Ray at home? I'd like to speak to him."

"He's right here, I'll get him. He's watching television with the children while I put supper on the table."

"I won't take long."

"No problem, take as long as you like. When are you coming to see us?"

"Maybe soon. We'll see," Mercita said.

"Good, Mom, we'll look forward to seeing you. Here's Ray."

"Hi, Momma! How are you?"

Mercita winced slightly hearing her son's voice, which she realized sounded so like the father he had yet to meet.

"I'm fine, Ray. Just a couple of things, how have you made out with the lawsuit?"

"Momma, I'm glad you asked. I was going to call you to let you know the case has been dismissed."

"Really? Everything's settled?"

"Yes, ma'am!"

"Oh Ray, I'm so glad. And in your favor?"

"That's right. Our lawyer made arrangements for the Marshalls to have two supervised visits with the girls, accompanied by a social worker. As a result of those meetings, a written report was submitted to the court. The social worker's reports indicated that the girls had already bonded to our family, were so confused by the appearance of two 'new' grandparents that they reacted unfavorably to the couple, and that in the best interests of the children they had already suffered enough with their mother's death…and, oh, a whole bunch of stuff. Anyway, the upshot was that the children are to remain in our custody, but the grandparents may visit them here at our house to try to get some kind of relationship going."

"Are they going to do that?"

"Who knows, Momma. The judge said they have to give us twenty-four hour notice if they're coming to visit."

"And how are the children doing?"

"They are fine. Kendra and I are relieved that the problem is behind us, we hope."

"I do, too, son."

"So, Momma, what's new with you? Doing ok?"

"I'm fine, son. Ray?" she took in a deep breath, "are you sitting down?"

"Sure, why?"

"I have something to tell you, and I'm afraid it may shock you."

"What is it?" he asked quickly. "You said you were all right…"

"I am, but I don't know how to tell you this, except to say it. I had lunch with your father today."

"My what? Momma, what are you talking about? My father?"

"Ray, son, it took him thirty-five years, but Win, your father, found me…and he wants to meet you."

Chapter Thirty-Six

Open house for Ariadne and Zachary's newly built home was in the planning stage. Ariadne and her mother were talking over the plans for the occasion.

As usual, they were having coffee in Ariadne's sparkling new kitchen.

"I do love this kitchen," Mercita said. "You're going to enjoy cooking here, the oak cabinets, and I do love the granite counter tops," she added.

"Zack designed it," Ariadne said.

"Did a real good job, I must say."

Mercita looked around the room with approving nods at what she saw.

"Honey," she said, watching for her daughter's reaction to her news, "I'd like to bring a guest along to your open house party."

"Mama!" Ariadne's face brightened with delight, "You've found yourself a boyfriend!"

"Not so fast, wait until I tell you who it is."

From her mother's tone of voice, Ariadne realized that her mother's news was serious.

"Ma? Who is it?"

Mercita sighed deeply, "Your brother's father, Winthrop Hatcher."

"Ray's father? After all these years?" Ariadne's eyes widened in disbelief.

"Yes, after all these years. He showed up in Connecticut. I've…well, I've seen him a few times."

"Mother!" Ariadne couldn't believe her ears. "You've been seeing him?"

"Yes, I have," her mother said. "As a matter of fact, he knows about you children, wants to meet both of you. I figure your housewarming would be a good time…"

"Well, I don't!" Ariadne broke in. "He hasn't been a part of your life for, what is it, thirty-five years! Look what he did to you…" Ariadne's anger was not totally unexpected, but her mother was surprised by the depth of her daughter's emotional outburst.

"Why, Mother?" Ariadne insisted, "Why would you allow a man you knew thirty-five years ago come back into your life? We don't need him to muddy up the water, disturb our lives, especially now that we're getting back on even keel. Things seem to be working out for all of us."

Mercita was silent for a moment because what her daughter had just said had already started to torment her. Did she need, want to renew a relationship that had its beginning so long ago, a lifetime ago?

When she had expressed that same doubt to Win, that a viable relationship was not a possibility, he had insisted that it was a distinct possibility and that his intention was to make their relationship a real one.

She reached across the table, pushed their half-empty coffee cups aside and reached for her daughter's hands.

"Child," she began, aware of the angry tension between them, "I have never loved you more than I do right now. And you know why?"

Tears flicked from her daughter's eyes as she shook her head no.

"It's because I know that you love me and want the best for me. That's why we can have these conversations. But as much as I love you, and I do, I gave you life, but I must make my decisions about my own life, whatever is left of it. And you must not be selfish, Ariadne, my dear. Think about your brother. What will it mean to him to have a father with whom he shares the same blood? That, too, is a decision he should have the right to make. Now that said, I will not bring Win to your home unless you and Zachary agree that he will be welcomed. I know that Ray has a lot on his plate right now resolving the custody battle over the girls, but he's going to meet his father and make up his own mind about whatever he wants to do. And when I decide what I am going to do, I'll let you know."

She cradled her daughter's tear-streaked face in her hands and kissed her.

"I've got to run now. Promised Ray and Kendra I'd have supper with them. In fact, I'm cooking supper for them tonight."

"What does Ray think about having a father turn up this late in his life?" Ariadne asked in a sarcastic tone.

"Doesn't know really what to think, but he does want to meet Win. And I believe he has that right."

✿

After her mother left, Ariadne sat at her kitchen table, idly twirling the half empty cup of cold coffee, thinking about her mother's shocking news, remembering the expression she had seen on her mother's face. An inner voice taunted her, even after thirty-five years of abandonment, my mother still cares about Winthrop Hatcher. How can she?

When Zachary arrived home that evening and was greeted with a perfunctory kiss, he stepped back to peer into his wife's troubled face.

"Honey, what's wrong?"

"It's my mother," she began.

"She's not sick, is she?" he said, anxiety in his voice.

"No, nothing like that. Ray…"

"Ray? What's wrong with him? I thought he and Kendra were doing fine."

"I guess they are."

"Well, what is it?" After years of dealing with distressed clients, Zachary realized his own wife was deeply upset. He led her to the sofa in the living room and sat down beside her. "Tell me," he said quietly.

Ariadne gave him a troubled look. "Ray's biological father has somehow turned up, out of the blue, has been in contact with my mother and...she wants to bring him to our housewarming..."

"That's great!"

Ariadne stared at her husband, disbelieving what she'd heard him say.

"You think it's great? After all those years...that he should just..." she stopped, seeing the disapproving look on her husband's face told her that he strongly disagreed with her.

"What? What?" she responded, disappointment and anger evident in her tone of voice.

"You think he has a right..." she persisted.

Zachary took her hands in his, realizing that his wife was indeed troubled, had been blindsided by the unexpected news. It was the first crisis that had occurred since their marriage and it was extremely important that he help her come to grips with the situation.

"Honey, there are 'rights,' and there are other 'rights'."

"You..." Ariadne could scarcely believe what her husband was implying.

"Wait, honey. Wait a minute!"

He rubbed his fingers over her knuckles softly and gently, seeking to lower the tension that gripped her.

"Your problem here is that you love your brother and your mother, and you don't want to see them hurt. That's what I love about you, Ari, you are a sensitive, caring person who wants to protect those she loves. And that is an admirable quality. But now you have to consider the rights, the desires, the decision of those involved, your mother, Ray, and his father. Ray has a right to respond to his father as he wishes, his father has a right to acknowledge his son, and your mother certainly has the right to continue or to sever her relationship to Win Hatcher as she chooses. If you love your brother, and I know you do, you must not be selfish. Think about what it will mean to him. How he must feel about being whole again, to have someone he belongs to, even after all these years. Does this line of reasoning make sense to you?"

She nodded her head, tears fell from her red-rimmed eyes onto their clasped hands.

Zachary took her in his arms.

"It's going to be all right. We'll invite them all to our housewarming, open up our hearts, as well as our home, and make everyone welcome. I love you, Ari..."

"You think I'm selfish?" Her tears continued and her quivering lips revealed the emotional tension she was feeling. "Don't you? I know you do."

"Not one bit! You are the most unselfish, giving person I know. I know deep down you want your mother and your brother to be happy. And from what you've said, your mother appears to want some sort of relationship with Ray's father."

"I…I think so. I haven't been told the whole story, except that years ago he went out on sea duty and when my mother found out that she was pregnant, she came east to her grandmother's to have Ray. She said that Win told her he searched for her. She told me that he said he looked all over for her, no one knew where she had gone. I believe my mother still cares for him. She said, 'After all these years, he found me. He said he never married because I was still in his heart!'"

"So, you can't hold it against him that they did not marry. I believe it was the circumstances of life that got in the way."

"I suppose you're right," Ariadne admitted."

"Right. And sometimes life leads us down an unknown path and we have to follow it, despite the twists and turns it presents to us. And, Ari," he said reflectively, "from what I've learned about your brother, Ray has the stamina and resilience to face whatever comes his way. Of that, I have no doubt. Come here…"

He gathered her in his arms, kissed the tears from her eyes.

"I only want everything to be right," she sobbed. "For, for my family…"

"And it will be. I promise," he said.

He was hoping that he could keep his promise to her, had already noticed how jittery and anxious she had become lately. He figured her tense restlessness was because of all the changes in her life, marriage, building a new house, furnishing it, designing it, and all the planning needed to complete the tasks, a great deal of which had fallen on her shoulders. He knew, too, how worried she was about her brother's custody problem. And now this latest development with Ray's father showing up. He made a decision.

"Look, hon, this has been a traumatic day for you. Why not call it a day, take a nice warm bath. I'll get it ready for you…"

"But supper…"

"Don't bother about supper. I'll order pizza and salad while you relax in the tub."

A few minutes later he told her, "Your bath awaits, madam."

"Zack, you're spoiling me," she smiled at him, still close to tears.

"My distinct pleasure. Allow me."

With a flourish, he opened the door to the bathroom.

The lights had been turned off. The room resembled a luxurious spa. The Jacuzzi jets bubbled softly, large fat candles on the shelf over the tub cast a warm glow over the room, and soft music from the intercom flowed seductively in the background.

"Oh Zack, how wonderful!"

He helped her into the tub. She lay back, rested her head on the toweled headrest, sighed deeply.

"This feels so good," she said as the scented bubbles rose up around her body.

Zack handed her a small glass of wine from a small table beside the tub.

"Enjoy," he said. He kissed her softly and left.

As she sipped the chilled wine the warm bubbling water caressed and soothed her body, tensions eased away and she realized how fortunate she was to have such a perceptive, understanding husband like Zack.

Chapter Thirty-Seven

It was Mercita who placed the call to Newport. She and Ray were seated side by side on the sofa in the living room of Ray's and Kendra's house. He had agreed with his mother that it was about time that he made some contact with Win.

"Hello, Win, it's me," she said into the phone. "I'm here in Ardmore with Ray and his family."

"Mercita!" Win's voice boomed over the phone. "How are you, and is everything all right?"

"Everything is fine. I am fine, and, yes, Ray wants to speak with you."

"That's great. I'm very anxious," Win told her. She could hear the tension in his voice.

Her eyes were wet with unshed tears and her voice was trembling with emotion when she handed the phone to Ray for the first exchange between the two most important men in her life.

"Son," she said, "the voice you'll hear next belongs to your father."

Without hesitation, his voice calm and firm, Ray spoke into the phone.

"Hello. I understand that you're my father."

"You understand correctly, sir. I, Winthrop Hatcher, am your biological father, and I am very anxious to meet you as soon as possible. Your wonderful mother has told me much about you and we've got to fill in thirty-five years as soon as we can."

Ray's reactions to the voice over the phone were somewhat ambivalent. His father's voice sounded affirming and confident rather than apologetic, as Ray had anticipated. So he was not prepared for the divergent feelings of acceptance and of suspicion that washed over him.

Since Letty's death he had endeavored to put his life on solid ground and felt that with Zachary's help and Kendra's love, he'd been able to do so. Now, this unexpected circumstance had been suddenly thrust into his life.

Deep down, he was excited. After all, he'd practically been struck by a thunderbolt. But he willed himself to speak in a calm manner to the man purporting to be his father.

"I understand, sir, that you have retired from the Navy and you live in Newport."

"Yes, I am retired, and at the present time I have temporary quarters at the Newport Harbor Island Hotel. Don't know yet where I'll settle…"

"That takes time, I guess, after being in the service so long."

"That's on hold for now, though I want you to know, Ray, that I consider myself one lucky guy to have found you and your mother after all these years." His voice sounded more positive as he continued to talk to his son. "Please, tell me about yourself. I want to know everything! I…I can't believe that I have a son!" he said. "Never in my wildest dreams…" his voice trailed off.

Ray heard a hesitant, choking sound as the man on the other end of the line seemed to be struggling with his emotions.

With his own feelings to deal with, Ray hesitated, not knowing quite what to say. Here was a man, a white man, that he barely knew existed, whose genetic code matched his own, whose voice sounded so much like his, and, as his mother had often told him, he so closely resembled. He scarcely knew what to say.

He took a deep breath and began to talk about himself.

✿

As Ray told his sister a few days later, "I didn't know what to tell the man. How do you talk to a complete stranger who brought you into the world?"

He had stopped by his sister's office to talk to her about the emotional conversation.

She was glad to see that he was beginning to look more like the brother she knew. Gone was the haggard, haunted look he'd had during the months after Letty's death. *Life with Kendra has made him happy,* she thought.

Her secretary had brought in a fresh pot of coffee with some homemade oatmeal cookies she had brought in to the office.

Ariadne poured a cup of coffee for her brother and offered it to him.

"Thanks, Sis. I need this, and I will have a cookie, too. Homemade, are they?"

"Right. Sara loves to bake, and she knew you'd be in today. So, tell me, how did it go, your conversation?"

"Well, we did talk. He sounded all right. Said he can't wait to meet me."

"How do you feel about that? Meeting him, I mean."

"I want to meet him. I don't know how I feel, Ari. Growing up without a dad, even though I loved your father, I always knew I was his stepson."

"He loved you like a son, Ray. You know he did."

"Yes, I did know that, but somehow this is different. It's a different feeling, considering that you're a creation formed by the love of two individuals. It's because of their love that I'm in existence."

He rubbed his forehead to wipe away the sweat that had collected as he continued to express his thoughts to his sister.

"I can't ignore that fact, no matter what I might think. Both of them, Mother and Win Hatcher, insist that untoward circumstances kept them apart. I can't ignore that."

"I understand that." She refilled his coffee cup, offered him another cookie that he declined with a wave of his hand. "Seems as if you've made up your mind…"

"I do want to meet him, Ariadne. Maybe I'm just curious, but, well, there's a part of me that wants to fill in the missing part, you know."

"How's Mama taking this?" Ariadne wanted to know.

"I think she's happy to know he's alive and well. She's excited for me to have a father and…"

"Think she loves him?" Ariadne broke in.

"Don't know. When she told me about him she was really quite emotional. I believe the fact that he's never married really touched her, you know. Never found another woman to take her place."

They were both silent for a few minutes. Ariadne stared out of her office window at the azure blue sky. Spring was fast approaching, the days were growing longer, the sun was much warmer, and she thought about her husband's comments he made when they had discussed her brother's situation.

She took a deep breath, turned her attention to her brother.

"I don't want you or Mama to be hurt, Ray. You know that. But whatever you want to do about this is up to you. You figure out whatever it is that you want, and whatever you decide will be all right by me. I know Mama would like to have him come to our housewarming party. When you meet him, please tell him we would like him to come."

"Thanks, Sis, I'll do that. I'm going to drive down Sunday, meet him at a restaurant."

"Nothing matters now except your happiness, yours and Kendra's. And, of course," she added, "Mama deserves only the best after all she's been through down the years."

"We're both lucky we've had such a strong role model in our lives," Ray said.

Ariadne agreed.

Chapter Thirty Eight

Ariadne was not prepared for the stunning feeling she experienced when her mother and Win appeared at the housewarming.

Her mother looked lovely in an emerald green, softly tailored linen suit. Her hair had been recently cut, her makeup soft and alluring. Ariadne thought she looked ten years younger since she had last seen her a month ago.

"Ari!" Her mother hugged her daughter, then turned to Win.

"Win, this is my daughter, Ariadne," Mercita said, maternal pride reflected in her voice.

Ariadne extended her hand to Win, who responded with a firm yet gentle gesture.

"It's nice to meet you," she said to him. "Welcome to our home. My husband, Zachary, will join us."

She was almost speechless when she realized that she was looking at an older copy of her brother. The resemblance between the two was clearly evident. This man, who carried himself with a military bearing, whose steel gray crew haircut was a carryover from his Navy years, whose slim, lean yet muscular body belied his age. He was wearing gray flannel slacks and a Navy blazer.

"Thank you for welcoming me into your home. I am honored. And please forgive me, but I have to tell you, you're truly your mother's daughter. Just as beautiful."

"Thank you. Please come in." She turned to see Zachary coming forward to greet the latest arrivals. Zack placed his arm around his wife, instinctively sensed her nervousness and sought to calm her by a gentle pressure of his hand on her shoulder.

"Mamacita!" he greeted his mother-in-law with a kiss on her cheek. "Good to see you again!"

Then he turned to Win, extending his hand. "I'm Zachary Richards, Ariadne's husband. Welcome to our home."

The two shook hands.

"I'm Win Hatcher. It's a pleasure to be in your beautiful home. Thanks for inviting me."

"Our pleasure," Zack said. "Come, have a look around."

He led them into the living room where the ocean could be viewed in its majestic glory through the expansive windows.

"We love this view" Zack said.

"It's very grand. I'm particularly delighted to be near the ocean. It's so special," Win admitted.

He turned to Ariadne's mother, who nodded her head in agreement. That's when Ariadne sensed the depth of the couple's commitment to each other. They were a loving pair, caring about one another without being overly sentimental or cloying. And she could see quite clearly that Win was certainly Ray's father. Their resemblance to one another was so unmistakable.

Zachary led them all to the back of the house to the solarium, a glass enclosed room where other guests had already assembled. He introduced Win to everyone by simply saying, "This is Win Hatcher, Ray's dad."

Ariadne noticed that her guests seemed to take the introduction quite well, accepting Win. Win and Ray greeted one another with hearty hugs and back-slappings.

Ariadne saw the look of happiness that crossed her mother's face and she knew then that her husband had advised her very wisely when he'd admonished her. "You are not responsible for the lives or the happiness of others in your family. You must live your own life and they must be allowed to do the same."

She knew then that whatever her mother wished to do about her relationship with Ray's father was up to her, but could she accept it?

Aridadne suspicions were confirmed. Dr. Lucas' broad smile when he helped her to a sitting position on the examination table said it all.

"You are about two months into your pregnancy. Your first, right?"

"Yes, but I hadn't really planned to have a baby this soon," Ariadne confessed.

"That's all right, they come when they come. You are in good health, and extend my congratulations to you and your husband."

When she left the doctor's office, her mind was flooding with images of babies. She was going to be a mother. New life, a new human being was alive because of the love that she and Zack shared. Her thoughts turned to her mother. How troubled she must have felt to bear a child alone without the support of the child's father, the man she loved.

Ariadne reached her car in the parking lot, got inside and sat quietly for a moment. Suddenly the enormity of her future overwhelmed her. What kind of mother would she be?

She fastened her seat belt, started the car, slowly backing out of the space. My family is getting larger all at once, it seems. Kendra, her son, Grady, Ray and the girls, Ray's father, Win Hatcher, and now the baby…and Mama, who started it all. Zack is right, I can't protect them all. Can't live their lives, only my own. I can't fix everything, as much as I want things to be right. Then, as she drove home, she realized that her wise husband's words had somehow relieved her of that enormous responsibility. She was free to live her own life, to love and support her family, but to allow them the freedom to live their lives as they wished. Her mother and Win, Ray and Kendra, did not need her counsel or advice.

Thirty minutes later she drove into the driveway of her home. A deep sense of peace and tranquility came over her as she viewed the home she and Zack owned and loved. Inside, the floor to cathedral ceiling windows of the living room welcomed her. She thought, in another seven months Zack and I will be bringing our newborn baby home.

Noting the time, she hurried into the kitchen to get supper ready. Zack should arrive anytime within the next half hour, depending on the evening traffic, and she could hardly wait to give him the news. She wondered if he had suspected she might be pregnant. He'd been so solicitous of her during her recent mood swings and emotional outbursts, like she'd had when she found out about Win Hatcher.

She sliced the leftover roast beef they'd had the evening before, placed the slices in a saucepan, added the gravy that she had made, and decided to warm up the rice when Zack got home. She was glad she didn't have to cook from scratch and that her husband was agreeable to leftovers. She put together a fresh salad, set the table, then she went into the bright, cheerful living room that she and Zack had designed to take advantage of the glorious ocean view from their expansive wall of windows. A wide green lawn and a cement wall separated the house from the ocean.

She plopped down on the large sectional sofa and stared out at the ocean. The tide was coming in and the majestic roar of the ocean's waves comforted her. A feeling of peace, well-being, an 'all's right with the world' sensation came over her. She looked around the well-appointed comfortable room, at the bookshelves that flanked the fireplace on the far wall, the African artifacts that Zack had collected placed about the room. It reflected the hopes and dreams they shared for the future.

She sighed deeply and laid her head back, closed her eyes. She was very fortunate. She had a wise and loving husband, a beautiful home, and now the baby that would complete their lives. The baby, she thought as she cradled her soft abdomen, a manifestation of the love that Zack and I share. The past, with its horrors, she thought briefly about the sexual attack, the problems with Ray's family, the return of Ray's father, all of those events were no longer her concern. She'd always want the best for her family, but she could no longer assume the responsibility for their well-being.

When Zachary came into the house twenty minutes later, he found his wife sound asleep on the sofa. He knelt down beside her, gently gathered her into his arms and kissed her.

"Wake up, Babe, I'm home."

Ariadne's eyes flew open. She flung her arms around her husband's neck. Her voice was thick with weariness.

"Zack! I'm sorry, didn't mean to…"

"It's all right, honey, you're overly tired, that's all. With the housewarming party, along with everything else, you've a right to be weary. You just lie here and rest. I'll take charge of everything."

"You're spoiling me, Zack."

"I'm supposed to, my sweet. It's an honor and a pleasure to do so. First thing, though, is to get a fire going in the fireplace."

He bustled around arranging the logs and kindling to his satisfaction.

"I want everything to be comfy and cozy for my lady," he told her with a broad smile.

"Your 'lady' loves the attention," Ariadne responded.

With the fire popping and crackling with lively bursts of color and flames, Ariadne's thoughts turned to the baby she carried, its life and its future. Please, God, she prayed, help me be a good mother and take away my shortcomings.

Then a tiny voice came unbidden, You can't be perfect. Just do the best you can.

Zachary came into the living room, arranged a tray table in front of her and returned with her food on a tray complete with silverware, napkin and a glass of wine.

Suddenly, Ariadne realized she was hungry, remembered she was now 'eating for two'. She wasn't sure about the wine, but made no mention of it to her husband.

Zack placed his own folding table beside hers and they sat side by side, eating and enjoying the crackling, cheerful fire.

"The roast beef is delicious, honey," he told her. "Don't know why, but it always seems better the second time around."

"It does," Ariadne agreed, and then she added, her eyes fixed on her husband's face, "Do you think my mother is going to marry Win Hatcher, Zack? I can tell she loves him."

"Honey, they have to."

"What do you mean, 'have to'?" she questioned, disbelief straining her voice. "What are you talking about, Zack?"

He laughed and gathered her close. "Not in the typical reference, sweetheart. What I mean is that the love I believe that they share is bigger than either of them. It wouldn't have lasted this long, thirty-five years, if it wasn't. It's as alive and as apparent as their relationship to their son. Anyone who is around them for a few moments can see it."

"I know, Zack. I certainly can. And Ray says he can, too, and somehow it pleases him. He said that when he and Kendra told Momma and Win that they are expecting a baby next fall, they thought Win was going to faint he got so excited! Couldn't believe that he was going to be a real grandfather. Both he and Ray are hoping it's a boy. Win plans on taking the child out on the sloop he's been working on, him and Ray."

"Seems to have brought them close," Zack observed. "The activity seems to have ratcheted up their comfort level with each other, so it wouldn't surprise me at all if Mamacita and Win tie the knot."

Ariadne nodded. "Zack, what if I told you that you are more than a husband?"

She looked directly into his eyes and said, "I mean it, Zack. You're much more than my husband. You're my best friend, my other half, and …you're the father of my child!"

The array of emotions that flickered over her husband's face when he took in what she was telling him gave Ariadne all the assurance she needed to verify her husband's love and commitment to her.

Awe, amazement, wonder, pride, elation, respect and adoration, it was all there and more in his face as he pulled her close.

"Oh my God, Ari," he choked. "Are you sure?"

She nodded, her eyes brimming with tears, overcome by her husband's reaction to her news.

"Dr. Lucas, I saw him this morning, sends you his congratulations…"

"When, Ari, when will the baby come?" Zack broke in.

"Around Thanksgiving."

"And you, you're feeling all right?"

"Fit as a fiddle. Dr. Lucas says I'm A-ok."

"Great! Have you told your mother yet?"

"Not yet. Wanted to tell you first."

"Come here," he held his arms open and she welcomed his embrace. Her head against his chest, his chin resting on top of her head, he whispered, "You're going to be the best mother in the world, I swear."

With her head pressed close to him, she heard the strong rhythms of his heart.

"If you'll help me, Zack, I promise to do my best."

His kiss said it all. Sweet, soft and sensuous at first, then responding to the eagerness and warmth of Ariadne's desire, Zachary pulled his wife to her feet, placing his arms beneath her, he carried her into their bedroom. Words were no longer necessary. Now was the time for the essence of their love to be shared.

"It's all right, babe?" he whispered as he lowered her to their bed, his eyes fixed on her lovely face.

"It's more than all right, Zack! I need you to love me, love me now!" Her eyes implored him and he sensed the depth of her feelings, her need to be loved, to feel secure. To feel desirable.

"Ari, you're so beautiful! So wonderful! You're much more than I deserve. I…I'm so lucky, so lucky," he murmured into her ear as he frantically tore off his shirt and trousers.

Anxious to feel his warm body next to hers, Ariadne twisted off her skirt and half slip, her cashmere sweater was flung to the floor. She lay in her bra and underwear, her eyes luminous and expectant as she waited for Zack to shed his briefs.

"You're sure, hon," he asked her. "This won't hurt you or the baby?" He leaned over to give her a gentle kiss.

"I'm very sure, Zack," she told him. She took his face into both of her hands and gently stroked the strong planes of his face.

"I know that I want you to make love to me, need you to love me, need…need your strength, your wisdom, your gentleness," she whispered softly.

She felt him release the clasp of her bra and heard his hissing intake of breath as the glorious orbs were released from their restraints, their roseate tips erect with sensual tension.

Moaning with uninhibited pleasure, her husband tasted the sweetness of first one then the other as Ariadne held him close. She felt that if she let go she might float off to some distant, far away place. She clung to Zack because her very life, she thought, depended on this moment. She felt that her body was melting, dissolving into nothing except for the soaring journey she was sharing with the man she was bound to love.

Zack's breathless excitement mingled with her own as the heat from their bodies flamed with delirious passion. Ariadne was not prepared for the emotional depths that churned wildly within her very soul.

She clung to Zack even more fiercely; digging her nails into his back as together they were thrust into the moment of exquisite joy.

"Ari, Ari, I love you," Zack whispered to her as slowly they both returned to normal breathing rhythms, still wrapped in each other's arms.

"Promise you always will," she whispered back.

"Always and forever, babe, and you know that, true as God, always and forever."

Ariadne sighed, placed her head on Zack's chest. His heartbeat returned to its normal steady beat reassured her. She loved a good man, she was loved, she was alive, and she carried a new life within her body. And she had Zack's promise of love everlasting. She needed nothing more.

Chapter Thirty-Nine

"Merci!" Win's voice boomed over the telephone, full of enthusiasm and boyish eagerness. Mercita remembered how eager Win had always sounded when excited. She heard it now in his voice.

"Yes, Win, what's happening?"

"Merci, I want to come down to Connecticut, pick you up and bring you here to Newport! There's something I want you to see!"

"Well, Win, I don't know. When were you planning on coming?"

"I know Tuesdays and Thursdays are your swim days, so how about Friday? Could we make it a weekend? I'll make a reservation for you here at the hotel. Please say you'll come. Can't wait to show you my surprise!"

"I…I'll have to think…"

"No, you don't have to think about anything," Win insisted. "I'll make the reservation for your weekend…and, oh, yes, you like jazz, I know. And, Merci, the Newport Jazz Festival is here. Supposed to be a great take-in. Not sure who's appearing, but it's usually some impressive artists. It will make a great weekend, Merci!"

"I have to be back here by Monday, at the latest. Not only for my swimming class…we're working hard on a new routine, you know, but I volunteer at the church's thrift shop Tuesday morning."

"Just like you, Mercita, always busy," Win said. "I'll be one happy person if you can squeeze in some time for me. We have so much catching up to do."

Mercita realized she felt drawn to Win, her love for him threatening to overwhelm her. Was that what she wanted…a relationship with the father of her son?

She knew she still cared a great deal for Win. Her heart soared every time he was near, but her brain was telling her to go slow…to be very careful.

Was she ready…to give up her present way of life to follow her heart once again?

"I do want to see you, Mercita, very much," he said over the telephone. His voice was filled with hope and expectation. Mercita made her decision. She spoke slowly, really to temper her own eagerness. She did want to be with Win.

"Tell you what, Win," she said. "Let me check, see if I can scout up someone to take my place at the thrift shop. I'll drive up. I want to check on Ariadne and Kendra, see how they're doing. Imagine, I'm going to be a grandmother of two!" she laughed. "Sure you want to be bothered with an old granny?" she teased.

"Are you kidding! You'll never be an 'old granny' in my book.

You're the most beautiful grandmother-to-be that I know."

"Flatterer!"

"Not flattery at all. It's the truth."

"Win, make the hotel reservation for the weekend, say Friday, with a check out for Monday morning. That way I should have time to see the children."

"Will do. But, Merci, you know I'd be more than happy to drive to Connecticut to pick you up. You don't need to drive up by yourself."

"I know that, Win."

"I know you, too, Merci," he interrupted. "You want to be independent so you can come and go as you please."

"Win, it's just that I've been independent so long."

"Well, we're going to have to make just a few minor changes in that status, m'dear," he said with a chuckle. "I'm so glad you're coming. Look forward to seeing you on Friday. Can't wait to show you my surprise."

✿

Win's surprise, as he called it, was at that moment floating at anchor in the blue-green waves that undulated against its sleek hull of teak and mahogany. When Win and Bill Harris drove to Joachim Alvares' home in Middleton, they were greeted by a large black dog with a coat of curly black hair. He ambled slowly toward the two men, definitive intelligence in his eyes as he recognized Bill Harris as a friend of his master.

"Portuguese Water Dog," Bill explained to Win as he bent down to greet the animal, scratch behind his ears.

Joachim, or 'Jack' Alvares, as he was most always known as, was of average height, solidly built, sturdy with dark eyes beneath shaggy eyebrows that seemed perceptive yet friendly. There were fine lined crinkles at the corners of his eyes. His skin had been browned and tanned, weather-beaten by his days and nights at sea during his occupation as a fisherman. His black, thick, curly hair was tinged along his temples with strands of steel gray. He was a very handsome man, Win thought. He was not surprised by the firm, warm handshake he received from him.

"Jack, want you to meet my new friend, Win." Bill Harris made the introduction.

"Win Hatcher," Win said. "I'm glad to meet you, Jack."

"Likewise, Win. Understand from Bill here that you'd like to take a look at my old sailing sloop."

"I'm really interested in it, if you want to sell it."

"Sure I do. Needs some work, but she's got a sound little body. Bill said you might want to do the work yourself." The three men walked down a long dirt driveway to the back of Jack's property. Through the trees Win could see the top mast of the boat bobbing up and down with the ocean waves. His heart beat triple time as they neared the wooden pier that stretched about fifty feet from the shore.

"There she is!" Jack Alvares exclaimed with an expansive gesture of his hand. "Ah, Jack, she's a beauty all right." Win grinned at the owner.

"Wait till you get aboard," Jack told him. "She's a thirty-six footer. What they call a sloop rigged sailboat. But you knew that, didn't you, just by looking at her."

Win nodded his head, almost unable to speak.

"I've put a new bottom on her, epoxy barrier. Her mast and rigging are new, put on last year. And in addition to new sails, I installed a 15 horsepower outboard. Come on, let's get aboard."

Don Carlos had already jumped over the gunwale of the boat, evidently quite at home in the environment.

"You'll see here," Jack pointed out to them, "besides her furled sails there's a full batten main white sail and the Genoa sail is white with red trim."

Win could see that both sails, although still furled, appeared to have been properly cared for. It looked seaworthy, but he knew he had to make a more detailed inspection. However, from the outset, he liked what he saw. A blue canvas bimini had already been installed over the large aft cockpit. He could already envision Mercita relaxing, enjoying what he enjoyed, a calm, serene life aboard a trim sailing vessel. He hoped with all of his heart to offer her that...and more.

Chapter Forty

Mercita had just returned home from her swim class.

"Mother," Mercita heard in her daughter's voice, a timbre she probably used with her clients. It was a formal tone of voice that meant the caller was in a serious frame of mind.

"Yes, honey, how are you feeling? Everything going ok?"

Mercita had answered with a matter-of-fact tone of voice, as if this were an ordinary regular call between mother and daughter. However, she was keenly aware of her daughter's ambivalence about Mercita's continuing relationship with Win Hatcher.

"I'm feeling fine, Mother. Are you all right?"

Well, Mercita thought, she's still concerned about me.

"I'm coming down to New Haven to attend a lawyers' conference at Yale. Thought I'd stop over and see you," Ariadne added.

"Oh, honey, that would be great! Is Zack coming with you?"

"No, he can't take time from his schedule, but I plan to drive down by myself."

"You feel up to that?"

"Of course, no problem."

"I'll be happy to have you, dear."

"I know, Mother, and you know we have to talk."

"Anytime. So when are you coming down?"

"The conference is on Friday, ten a.m. to three p.m. So I plan to get to your house between four and five, depending on the evening traffic."

"That will be great. I'll have supper ready when you get here. Be careful and...my best to Zack"

As she hung up the phone, Mercita had realized that the future relationship between her and her daughter might very well hinge on this impending visit.

Friday turned out to be a delightful June day. The weather was sunny and mild, with little wind. The colorful flowering trees like magnolia, dogwood and cherry, the bright azaleas all added a festive, joyous feeling to the environment.

As she had gone about her preparations for her daughter's visit, Mercita had prayed that the weather augured a reasonable compromise.

The day before she had shopped for food and had planned a simple meal of roast lamb, Ariadne's favorite roast, asparagus spears, wild rice with herbs, a simple green salad, mint jelly, and for dessert a strawberry chiffon pie decorated with sliced strawberries and whipped cream.

Ariadne had arrived a little before five. Her mother had welcomed her with open arms in a warm hug. She took her daughter's briefcase and overnight bag from her and took a few steps back to look her child over.

"Honey, how are you feeling? What is it, about three months now? I see you're not in maternity clothes yet."

Ariadne sighed as she took off her suit jacket, laid it on the chair beside the hall table.

"I'm feeling ok. No more morning sickness, and I'm still wearing my regular clothes," she said as she pressed both hands over her lower abdomen. "Just have a little pouch right here."

"Well, you do look great to me. Come on in, dinner's ready. You can freshen up while I start dishing up. Hope you're hungry."

"It smells good, Momma, and I am hungry. As they say, I'm eating for two!"

Back in her kitchen, Mercita had thought about her daughter. Would she be able to answer questions about her relationship with Win when she didn't know herself exactly how she felt about him?

She retrieved the already prepared salads from the refrigerator, placed them on the dining room table in a corner of her large living room. Then she filled two dinner plates with slices of lamb, asparagus spears, a serving of wild rice, placed them on the placemats while she waited for her daughter.

When Ariadne finally came in and sat down at the table, her mother brought in a bowl of hot gravy and a pitcher of iced tea.

"Good to have you here, honey. Tell me, how is Zack reacting to his impending fatherhood?"

"Oh, he's thrilled to death. Can't do enough for me. I just talked to him on my cell phone…said to tell you hi."

"You tell him hi back for me, and tell him that it pleases me that he is good to you. I remember how special your father treated me when we were expecting you. I could hardly breathe the words, 'I need or I want,' before your father was trying to grant my every wish."

Ariadne looked at her mother, a frown tracked across her forehead.

"Momma," her voice was soft and low. "Did you love my father?"

Mercita answered solemnly, "With all my heart. More than you'll ever know. He was a wonderful person."

"Then why?"

"Why what?" Mercita asked, knowing full well what was on Ariadne's mind.

"Why are you continuing this relationship with Win Hatcher? If you loved my father, how can you do that?"

Mercita cut a bite sized piece of meat, put it in her mouth, chewed slowly before she swallowed. She took a sip of her iced tea, then she answered her daughter.

Before she could say anything, Ariadne blurted out, "I just can't stand it! He abandoned you, left you pregnant, like all white men think they can do whatever they like…"

"You're dead wrong, honey. Win did not attack me nor hurt me at all. We loved each other and I shared an expression of that love with him, the man I loved. It was the ultimate experience that awakened me, to be loved by a wonderful man, and that night gave me a son. And as hard as my life was at that time, I have never regretted having had that one glorious experience. Some women never know love, but I have been loved by two extraordinary men."

"But, Mother, Win is white!"

"That's not his fault. He is what he is. I never noticed…"

Then Mercita saw a dark look cloud over her daughter's face.

What? What is it?" she demanded, dreading what she might hear. What was bothering the child?

"I was attacked by a white man." Ariadne blurted out in a rushed tone of voice as if she could not hold back another moment.

Startled by the news, Mercita reached for her daughter's hand.

"Oh, honey! When? You never told me…"

"It happened during law school. I didn't tell you because I thought the same thing had happened to you."

"Did you ever find out who did it? That's a dreadful experience to go through."

"No, I never did. Just put it in the back of my mind."

"No wonder you mistrust Win. But I assure you, Win would never harm me."

"But, but he left you…"

"No, he did not! He was sent away on sea duty. I never knew how that came about. We had planned to get married, but…"

"And now?" Ariadne persisted.

"I'm not sure. Listen, does Zack know about this assault?"

"I told him before we were married, had to because I wanted…" she hesitated.

"I understand…you wanted only the best for him. What did he say when you told him?"

"That I had been criminally assaulted, that my peace of mind had been stolen from me and that…that he would always love me."

"He's right, you know. No wonder I love that boy. Did you see a doctor?"

"When it first happened, I did see the school physician. She was very good to me. I've had regular gyn follow-ups, and Mother," Ariadne smiled slightly as she told her mother,.

"And that was important to you, honey. I know it was."

"Silly of me, Momma, with all the sexual freedom and the relaxed mores of the times. I don't know why I am such a prude, but, well, I guess I am."

There was a silence between them as they continued to eat. Finally, Mercita spoke up. She wanted to reassure her daughter.

"My dear child, you were always, always trying to be perfect. Always wanted your hair to be braided just so, always trying to please me and your father, never wanted to get your clothes dirty. Always looking out for your brother, which you continue to do to this day. Your father and I worried about you trying to reach the unattainable...perfection. It's not for us humans, and we were delighted when as you grew up you relaxed and matured to become the warm, loving, caring young woman we loved so much. We were very happy."

"Guess I was a handful, eh?"

"You could say that, hon. But I'm proud of you. Ray, too. You're both wonderful children. I don't deserve to be so lucky."

Ariadne reached across the table to hold her mother's hand.

"Don't say that, Momma. We're the lucky ones. I just don't want you to be hurt. By Win or anyone else."

"I know, and I'll tell you this," Mercita said as she squeezed Ariadne's hand, "I can tell you I don't really know how my relationship with Win is going to turn out. Really, I don't know. I do know that Win is ecstatic over the discovery of his son, your brother...says it is the most wonderful thing, something he never expected. So..."

"I just don't want you to be hurt, Momma. You know what I mean," Ariadne interrupted.

"Yes, honey, I do know. But you must go on with your own life. Be happy with Zack and your baby, because when that child gets here, it's going to bring with it a love stronger than you could imagine. Believe me, I know. And, Ari, my dear, dear daughter, don't you worry about me. I'm going to be just fine, with or without Win."

She laughed at her own little joke, walked around the table where her daughter sat and hugged her. She rested her chin on top of Ariadne's head.

"As soon as I know, I'll let you know."

Chapter Forty-One

Now, a week later, riding in the car with Win to see his surprise, she wondered herself if she did have a future with this man who had re-entered her life.

She watched as Win's strong, capable hands maneuvered the steering wheel to drive right onto a side street. She remembered them as being gentle, caressing hands, and she shook her head slightly to chase away the memory.

Win noticed the gesture, asked, "Are you all right, Merci?"

"I'm fine."

"Well," he assured her, "we're almost there."

"It's been a lovely drive so far, Win. So glad to have summer weather back again."

"I now what you mean. Last winter was dreadful. But we're going to enjoy the rest of the summer. This I guarantee."

The lighthearted tone in his voice added to his boyish animation. Mercita hoped she would react properly when she saw whatever it was that had so enlivened and excited him.

"I just had to show this to you first, Merci, before I shared it with anyone else. I Can't wait to see your reaction."

He drove slowly down the street, searching for Jack's house.

"You've got me all excited, Win, I can tell you that. Can't wait to see what has got you so fired up."

He turned into Jack Alvarez's driveway, went past the house and onto the dirt road that led to the wooden pier.

"This is it," he said to Mercita as he turned off the ignition. "We're here."

He opened her car door to help her out. Holding her hand, he walked her down to the pier and pointed to the sailing sloop that rocked at anchor, back and forth, swaying gently as quiet waves lapped against her hull, "what do you think of that! Is she a surprise or not?" He grinned, waved his hand at the boat.

He was pleased when he saw a soft flush come over her face and her dark eyes sparkled with delight. He had hoped to see just such a reaction from her. A brief memory of their earlier days as young lovers flickered into his mind. They had been so carefree and happy then. Could it be possible to recapture a little of that ecstasy they had once shared? Silently, he vowed to do all that he could to make it happen.

With a boyish grin, he asked, "What do you think of that?"

"Win! You didn't! You bought this boat?"

"I sure did," he smiled. "This is my very own sailing sloop. I'm going to call her Sweet Merci of the Sea. Decided that when I retired I'd find a sailboat that I could maybe do a little work on. Something that would keep me busy. I've spent most of my life on the water and really, it's where I'm most comfortable. Would you like to go onboard?"

"I would," she smiled, suddenly eager to share in his enthusiasm.

"I've got you," Win assured Mercita as he helped her maintain her balance. ""She looks very well-cared for," Mercita said, rubbing her hand along the teak gunwale. She sensed Win's pride in the trim little boat. She saw the boyish delight in his face, like a teenaged boy with his first car. She found herself moved by his apparent happiness.

Win's hand under her elbow steadied her as he made the rounds, pointing out to her the various features of the sloop.

"Her mast is new, and the riggings are, too," he showed her. There's a tiny galley below with a small two plate burner, refrigerator and sink. The head, toilet to you, m'dear, is forward of the galley. She sleeps four, and with the long shaft outboard, can move up to six and a half knots."

"But you want to sail her most of the time, don't you, Win?"

"I do, but it's a plus to have the power if you have no wind for sailing," he advised.

"Is it hard? Sailing, that is."

"Gosh, no. I started when I was a kid. My folks gave me a little sunfish when I was about seven and I learned how. Spent most of my summers sailing Newport harbor. Think you'd like to learn to sail? Bet you'd be an excellent sailor."

"Think so?" She smiled at him, a girlish tilt to her head.

He responded quickly, delighted with her enthusiasm. "I do. You're a wonderful swimmer. And I'm certain you'd be comfortable on the water. In no time I could have you weighing anchor, get under way and head out to blue water. I know you could pick it up in no time. And," he added, "I'd love to be your teacher. We'd have great fun together."

"Well, maybe I could. Always said that it never hurts to learn new skills."

He led her aft to the deck covered by the blue canvas bimini. He pointed upward.

"This keeps the sun off you when sitting out here. I'm getting some canvas deck chairs and a couple of small tray tables so we can enjoy snacks out here."

"How much work is involved, Win, in getting things the way you'd like?" she asked.

"Not too much. I'd like new seat cushions."

"I could help with that," she interrupted. "I have a sewing machine."

"Good. I want to check over the steering wheel, make certain it's in good working order, all the winches and the rudder. There's always some hands-on work when you own a boat, you know. But you do like it, don't you, Merci?"

"I really do, Win. And I'm so glad for you, that you're happy."

Chapter Forty-Two

As they returned to the car, Mercita told Win that she would like to get back to the hotel, she needed to call her children to let them know that she was in Newport and would be coming to Boston. She wanted to see for herself how the two pregnant girls were doing. Win's excitement over becoming a grandfather pleased her. He was like the young man she had loved years ago, warm, spirited, enthusiastic about life. She realized, too, that he was able to make her feel the same way.

"You're sure you don't mind, Win?" she asked him.

"Fine with me, Merci. Whatever your heart desires. It's just so wonderful to have you here by my side." He leaned over and kissed her cheek. "I'm warning you, Merci, I'm going to do all in my power to see that you stay right here. I want to get back some of what we had. It's not too late, you know."

He turned on the ignition, shifted gear and backed slowly away from Jack's house. "Nice guy." Win commented.

"I know."

"I love and respect you, Mercita. I really do. I admire your independence, your courage, and I love you. Always have, always will." Win wasn't sure where that came from, but he was glad he said it.

"Well, you made me very happy today when you said a 'real father will never deny his child.' I want you and Ray to respect and love each other. That's all I ask."

Win saw moisture shining in Mercita's eyes as she made her plea.

"Honey, I'll do all in my power to make your wish come true. I promise."

As he drove he remembered the early days when they were young lovers. They had been so happy then, unencumbered, free to love each other. Their forced separation had been so hard; could they re-capture some of that happiness again?

They arrived back at the hotel around five that afternoon. Mercita went immediately to her room, promising Win that she would meet him in the lobby for dinner at eight.

She took a shower, shampooed her hair and blow dried it. Glad that she had just had a hair cut, her crisp, short gray curls framed her face and she was pleased with the reflection she saw in the mirror. She wondered, did she look fifty-five to Win? For her, Win seemed almost as she remembered him. He was still slim and lean as he used to appear in his sparkling navy whites. His age was evident only by the glints of silver in his close cropped hair and the fine crinkle-like lines around the corners of his eyes whenever he smiled. As she thought about him, the natural love, concern and pride he showed toward their son, a warm feeling of contentment began to form deep within her. It seemed to be a feeling of hope, of peace, as if her tilted world had somehow righted itself and was revolving at a comfortable gratifying pace that calmed her, eased her body and soul.

She sighed, picked up the phone and dialed her daughter's number. As she listened, waited for her daughter to answer, she tried to prepare herself for what she expected would be Ariadne's reaction to her call. Honesty and respect had always been maintained between mother and daughter. Mercita had raised both her children with that precept. Her grandmother always said, "Where there's understanding and respect, there is love."

After the fourth ring she heard a cheerful hello which pleased her. 'Hi, honey, it's me!"

"Momma, how are you?"

"I'm just fine, but how 'bout you? How're you feeling?"

"I'm doin' fine. Doctor says everything's right on schedule."

"Wonderful! And Kendra? How's she making it?"

"Doing very well. We have the same doctor, you know, Dr. Lucas. Understand that he and his staff have bets on which one of us will deliver first. Our due dates are close, you know."

"Wouldn't it be something if you both delivered the same day."

"You just plan to be around, Momma."

"Wild horses wouldn't keep me away, honey."

On that last word, Mercita thought she'd better get to the reason for her call.

"Ariadne, honey, I'm coming up to see both of you, check on you with my own eyes. I'm here in Newport, see, and…"

"Newport! What are you doing in Newport?"

"Visiting Win. He invited me to spend the weekend with him."

"Mother! Spend the weekend! Are you out of your mind?"

Mercita was not surprised by her daughter's dismay. She said, "Ah, remember, honey, when we had our 'talk' a while back and I said that as soon as I knew what was in my heart, you would be the first to know…"

"How can I forget?" Ariadne answered, distinct resentment in her voice.

Mercita took a deep breath as if to prepare herself for the inevitable onslaught she had anticipated from her daughter.

Chapter Forty-Three

Ariadne wasn't surprised over her concern about Ray's father's reunion with their mother.

Zack's initial response was, if happiness comes your way, embrace it.

But she did not see it that way. She had to call her mother once more, make her see the folly of such a relationship...after all these years.

So she phoned. Would she be able to make her mother see reason?

"I can certainly understand your wanting to have him as a friend, Momma, but how can you care for someone who left you...to have a baby all by yourself?" Ariadne persisted over the phone.

"On the contrary, my child. I think I'm in love," was Mercita's response to her daughter's query.

Over the phone, Mercita heard her daughter's hissing intake of breath as she blurted out, "Mother!"

Mercita answered quickly.

"No, that's not right! Honey, I don't think I'm in love with Win, I know I am and I've never been happier."

Mercita thought, what a day this has been. One I never expected.

She answered Ariadne's objections the only way she knew how, with sincere honesty.

"Ariadne," she spoke clearly and slowly, gripping the phone as hard, as fierce as she had gripped the bedrails when she gave birth to her daughter, "listen to me. You know there is nothing, nothing I won't do to make you happy, except for this...my own happiness. I have an unalienable right to happiness and I intend to find and cherish that happiness if it comes to that."

"But..." Ariadne interrupted.

"No buts. I know you're going to ask me again if I loved your father. I did, with all my heart. He was a wonderful husband to me, and I take none of that from him. He will always, you hear me, always have his place in my heart. As for Win, where he is concerned, the love between us has survived thirty-five years of separation, of yearning, of hope, and we're looking forward to at least thirty-five more. And, by the way, Win did not leave me pregnant and barefoot. He did not know about the baby because I didn't know either, so I couldn't tell him."

Mercita drew a deep breath and exhaled audibly as she waited for her daughter's response. The silence between them was deafening.

"I do understand, Momma," Ariadne said softly. "I only want what's best for you. You deserve to be happy."

"Honey, I've never been happier. So, shall I come up for a visit? I want to see Kendra and Ray, too."

"By all means, please come. And, Momma," Ariadne's voice softened as she added, "bring Win, too. Tell him I want him to come. Will you do that, Mother?"

"Of course I will."

Mercita replaced the phone into its cradle, her palms wet and sweaty. She went into the closet to pick out something to wear, get ready to meet Win for dinner. She wondered if she had been too harsh with her daughter. But as far as she was concerned, it was all a matter of life, one's own life, and the right to pursue one's personal happiness. Surely, as an expectant mother, Ariadne's own joy could allow latitude for the happiness of others.

Mercita decided to wear a black silk pants suit that night. A rose colored silk blouse with a large soft bow at her neckline brought warm tones to her face. For her jewelry she placed the diamond studs that her late husband had given her into her earlobes. Black satin pumps with a moderate heel and a black thin shoulder strap purse completed her outfit. She spritzed a little of her favorite perfume behind each ear, grabbed her purse, room key, and proceeded to the bank of elevators.

As she sat in the lobby waiting for Win to arrive, she knew she was early, but she wanted to be. She looked around the well-appointed lobby. The glass atrium in the center soared majestically skyward. Tall graceful tropical trees rose aloft as well. Great bronze urns held ferns and exotic plants. Huge porcelain vases, obviously brought from China by the sea captains who had opened the China trade were placed about the lobby. It was a luxurious room with oriental carpets, sofas with deep leather cushions. Mercita could understand a Navy man's preference for a hotel like Newport Harbor.

As she waited for Win, her thoughts drifted back to their earlier days…their discovery of each other and the love that grew between them. She never forgot the joy, the harmony she felt when they were together. She was like a harp, her body vibrated with heart-felt passion whenever Win touched her. "Life is good," he had whispered to her. "Our love is true, real. I want you to be with me, by my side, forever, Merci," he had said as his mouth traveled all over her body, loving it, bathing it with love. Her memories of that night, now she knew it was the night their son was conceived, were as fresh in her memory as if they had occurred the previous night. Suddenly her eyes filled with tears as she realized that was when her innocence had been lost forever. Everything was different now. She was even about to become a grandmother. Should she trust the emotions that had exploded that afternoon and let Win into her life again? She'd just about told her daughter that she was going to do so. Did she mean it? There would be no going back. Should she go forward with

Win? Was that what she really wanted? Did she deserve it?

She blinked, reached for a tissue in her purse, had just wiped her eyes dry when she saw Win enter the lobby. His warm smile when he spotted her erased the niggling doubts that had pestered her. Thirty-five years were past, forgotten, her feelings for this man were the same. They rose up within her. She could not deny them. She welcomed the sweet caress of his lips on hers as he bent over to kiss her.

"You look so beautiful, Merci." He took her hand, led her toward the dining room.

His black blazer, sharply creased gray slacks, gave him a somewhat formal look, but the white turtle-necked jersey he wore tended to lessen the severity of his attire.

Mercita placed her arm in the crook of Win's elbow, calmed by the warmth of his body through the soft wool of his sleeve.

The maitre'd led them to their table. "Tonight's special is rack of lamb, or a seafood casserole," he told them as he handed each a menu. "Of course, there are other entries if you'd care to check."

"Just give us a moment," Win told him. "But a bottle of your best wine, chilled, please."

"Right away, sir," the man said.

"Well, now, Mercita, it's been quite a day. I'm so glad you're here with me."

"I'm enjoying myself, Win," she said as she fingered the stem of her wine glass. "I'm happy to see you so excited about your boat."

He grinned at her, and she could almost see the twenty year old she had loved so deeply years ago. She inhaled a deep breath as she delighted in his stark good looks. His skin reflected a healthy glow, tanned and weathered, no doubt by his many days at sea. His wide smile that made his eyes sparkle, crinkle gently at the corners, welcomed her. She sighed, exhaled slowly.

Win noticed and reached across the table to take her hand.

"What is it, Merci? What's troubling you?"

She rubbed her thumb over his knuckles. His skin was warm and dry.

"Win, would you mind too much if we skip the jazz festival tomorrow?"

"Gosh, not at all. Whatever you wish, it's okay by me."

"Well, would you mind going with me to Boston tomorrow? I'd like to check on the two expectant mothers."

He gave her a wide grin.

"Mercita, I'd love to go! Give me a chance to see Ray, tell him about the boat. I have pictures of it that I'd love to show him. Hope I can interest him in working on it with me. I'd love to go see the family. Are you kidding me, of course we'll go to Boston! Not a problem at all, sounds like a better idea than any old jazz festival!"

Chapter Forty-Four

It was Ray who called his sister a few days later after Mercita and Win had visited that weekend.

"Feeling good, Sis?" he asked her when he telephoned.

"Feeling fine, Ray. Can't see my feet when I stand up, I'm as big as a house. But how 'bout Kendra? How's she doing?"

"Good. She says she's feeling just fine. She told me this pregnancy is easier than her first. I'm glad of that. Say," he wanted to get right to the point, "did you notice anything different about Momma last weekend?" he asked his sister.

"You mean other than looking twenty years younger? Made me feel like an old hag, big belly an' all."

"Ari, she's in love. Don't be surprised if she and Win get married."

"Did either of them say anything about getting married?"

"Didn't need to."

"It would mean a lot to you, Ray, wouldn't it?" Ariadne said quietly.

"Yes, I believe it would."

"I would never stand in the way, Ray. Like I told Momma, it's her happiness that I care about, the whole family's really. And like my beloved husband has reminded me, you can live only your own life, not the lives of others. Momma's a tough cookie, she's been through a lot, but she's a survivor and I do want to see her happy."

"I think she's going to find it...with Win, my...my father."

Ariadne heard distinct pride in her brother's voice.

"I believe you're right, Ray."

Because it was Tuesday, Ariadne knew her mother would not be at home until later in the evening. Zachary was at the board of directors meeting for one of the local colleges, so she decided she would place her call to her mother before he returned home that evening.

It was nine o'clock when she dialed her mother's number in Connecticut.

"Momma, how are you?"

"Oh, Ari, I'm just fine. How are you?"

"Big as a house. Just sitting around 'nesting' like some big bird."

"And Zack, how's he doing?"

"He's doing well, he's so excited about the baby. He's at a meeting right now. I expect him home any minute now. But, Momma, I'm really calling to tell you...well, to tell you, that is, Ray and I talked today about you and Win. We both could tell how happy you looked, and like I told Ray, you seemed twenty years younger."

"I did? You thought I looked young?"

"Sure did. We both did. And…we both realized that it was because you are happy, so," Ariadne drew in a deep breath, "I say go for it! You sure don't need my permission at all, but I want you to be happy, so I say you and Win should get married if that's what you want. And the sooner the better, before your grandbabies get here."

"Oh, honey, thank you. Ray agrees, too?"

"He wants it very much. He won't be in limbo anymore, he said."

Win's regular ten o'clock call came shortly after Mercita had concluded her talk with Ariadne. She was feeling relaxed and happy after her conversation with her daughter. Not that she needed the child's approval, but her relief knew no bounds because finally Ariadne had accepted reality.

"Yes, Win, I'm here. The swim class? Went off without a hitch," she told him in answer to his question. "Yes, Jack Hunter is pleased with the way we 'girls' have mastered the new routine." Mercita laughed. "He says we're the best in the world, but then he always says that. What's that, Win?"

She listened to his question, slipped her shoes off and stretched out on her bed. Her hair was still slightly damp from her swimming session and she was anxious to get ready for bed.

"Yes, Win, I am ready. My bag is packed, my passport is in order, and I've asked my friend to keep an eye on my house, collect any newspapers, mail. Although I've requested that those be held, you never know. I'll be ready in the morning, but if you don't let me get some sleep, I'll be a bleary-eyed old woman!"

She smiled at his protests as her heart thumped wildly in her chest. When she returned to this bed again, she thought Win will be with me and I will be Mrs. Winthrop Hatcher.

Win had arranged everything. The wedding coordinator of the cruise ship assured him when he contacted her that the ship's chapel would be appropriately decorated, the music he had requested would be supplied, witnesses to the private ceremony from the executive staff would be present, as well as a clergyman to perform the service. All that was needed was the bride and groom. The coordinator had even provided a young woman, part of the crew, to assist Mercita, who welcomed the competent help.

The ceremony was brief and went off without any difficulty.

When the clergyman asked about their vows, Win pulled a white card from his jacket pocket. In a firm, but quiet voice he read, 'Dear Mercita, love led me to you, kept you safe all these years until I could find you again. We are now to be one, finally, with all our promises to keep.

Everything in life is possible with you at my side. My heart, my whole being is in your hands. Will you be my wife?'

Mercita responded by saying, "Win, I accept your love with my whole being. Your love is the soft breeze that caresses me, freshens and sustains me. I affirm my love for you with all that I am or shall ever be. Win, I will be your wife."

Then they exchanged rings and recited their final vows.

They had dinner that evening at the captain's table, after which they were invited up to the bridge. The wedding coordinator had arranged the special invitation upon learning of Win's naval career. Win was delighted to have the opportunity to show his wife the naval instruments and intricate machinery needed to propel and navigate the cruise ship. It was a starry moonlit night on the ocean as they sailed toward their honeymoon destination on one of the small Caribbean islands. They stood on the stern deck, arm in arm, as they watched the frothy wake from the stern of the ship.

"It's been the most wonderful day, my Mercita," Win told her as he took her in his arms. He kissed her then and she felt like a young bride again because this man had been her teacher, the one who taught her love. She returned the kiss, astonished by the hunger her own body seemed to feel, the need that had been unmet for so many years. Now she could savor, react, reclaim what had been taken from her so many years ago. She never dreamed she would experience this love ever again.

As if he could read her mind, her husband said, "You must be tired, honey. It's been a long but exciting day. Would you like a drink before we turn in?"

"I don't think so, Win. I'm already wired up enough. It's been a wonderful day, husband of mine," she patted his cheek, "and I'm looking forward to many more."

"Sweeter words I've never heard," Win said as he led her inside. Music could be heard coming from one of the lounges and the sound reverberated in his heart with joy and delight. For the first time in his life he was supremely happy.

When he and Mercita got into the elevator, Win pressed the signal button to go up to the sky deck.

"Shouldn't we be going down to B deck?" Mercita asked.

With a big grin on his face he reached, pulled her close. "Not to worry. We're upgraded to the bridal suite on sky deck."

"But, but, my luggage, my clothes…"

"Everything has been taken care of," he reassured her.

"We're here," he said as the elevator came to a stop. They walked down a thickly carpeted corridor toward a red door decorated with a pair of golden love birds. "One moment," Win said as he opened the door.

With the key safe in his pocket, he picked Mercita up, carried her over the threshold into the suite of rooms that took Mercita's breath away.

"Win, it's beautiful!" Mercita said, her arms around his neck. Fresh flowers decorated the well-appointed living room. Soft lights enhanced the setting, creating a feeling of luxury and comfort.

"I'm glad you like it. Let's check out the master bedroom."

A tray of chilled sandwiches, assorted cheeses, crackers, fresh fruit, nuts, candies, as well as small tea cakes and tarts had been placed on a serving tray beside the bed.

"We're not going to starve, I see," Win pointed out to Mercita.

"Not hardly," she agreed. She walked into the bathroom.

"Win!" she called out to him, "there's a spa-sized tub in here big enough for a family of four."

He reached her side and drew her close. "Let's start with a family of two. Just us, Mrs. Hatcher."

But a hot tub was not what either one of them wanted. And they knew it.

When Win came to their bed after his shower, Mercita opened her arms to welcome him.

He kissed her, slid naked beneath the cool, smooth sheets, drew her warm, silk-like body close to his. He whispered into her ear, "Mercita, it's been so long, so long since I've held you like this. We've got so much to make up for."

"Don't talk, Win. Love me, please. You do love me, don't you?"

He talked with his lips close to hers.

"I do love you, Merci. I'll die loving you." His mouth closed over hers and she felt a hot, melting sensation creep from the center of her body outward to her extremities and the resulting flames that singed her, burned her flesh made her cry out as if in pain. She was no longer a mature woman, or about-to-be-grandparent. She was a flesh and blood woman. Win's loving touch peeled back the years and she was again the eager young woman tasting the sweetness of love for the first time. She had known it would be like this. Thirty-five years ago Win's love had plucked at the strings of her heart. The feeling was still there, only deeper, more intense. She wanted him, needed him to verify her reason for living. Her joy was so great, tears squeezed beneath her closed eyelids. Quickly, Win kissed the moisture away, whispering, "It's all right, love, don't cry. It's been a long time but we're together at last. Nothing nor no one can separate us, ever! I promise I will always love you. Always."

As if to verify his words, his strong, sensitive fingers gently cupped one of her soft, still delicately mounded breast while his mouth greedily sought a response from her other. Unhurriedly he continued his exploration of her body until a silken sheen of dew-like moisture covered her body. Its golden hue enchanted Win. "My very own beautiful goddess," he murmured softly.

Mercita's body began to tremble, her head moved frantically from side to side as she tried to free herself from her exquisite agony. Win stretched his body over hers. "You are more beautiful than ever, Merci, mine. I love you so much."

With the firm pad of his thumb, he touched the moist, extremely sensitive core of her body. Mercita's reaction was a stunning arching of her whole body, and she panted in short breaths as if she had been burned. She whimpered, begged, "Please, Win, please."

The moment for fulfillment had finally reached them. They welcomed its arrival with muffled cries of ecstatic joy as their cruise ship crested the ocean's waves to bear them to their long sought after destination of love.

Epilogue

Dr. Lucas peeled off his rubber gloves, tossed them into the appropriate discard box, stripped away his blue scrub gown and announced to his team, "One down, one more to go!"

He was answered by his assistant, who was finishing up with the new mother, "Way to go, doc! Way to go!"

"You know, don't you, Chet, that I'm getting too old for these 'back to back' deliveries. Soon's you finish up here with Mrs. Hatcher, come over to the next delivery room. Mrs. Richards is fully dilated and ready to push."

He hurried out the double doors to the adjacent delivery room.

"Well, are we ready?" he asked the weary, tired mother-to-be.

"I'm ready, and I sure hope you are, too," his patient replied.

Dr. Lucas turned to the patient's husband, clad in sterile cap, mask and scrub suit. He shook hands with the man.

"Let's have us a baby!"

Groups of excited relatives, aunts, uncles, grandparents, as well as assorted siblings crowded around the nursery viewing window, admiring the new additions to their respective families.

One tall man with steel gray hair whispered to his wife, "I can't believe it! Two grandchildren born within an hour of one another! It's amazing!"

His wife agreed, smiled up at him.

"You owe me fifty dollars, you know. I told you Kendra would deliver before Ariadne."

His face sobered as he looked at her. Oblivious to the people around them, he took her face in his hands. "I owe you much more than fifty dollars, my dear. I owe you my family, my life, and my eternal happiness."

"I must say, husband mine, it took you over thirty-five years to 'make a family', but when you finally do it, you do it real well!"

She grasped his arm and they walked down the hospital corridor to greet the new mothers who shared a double room.

They stopped before entering the room.

"Win, do you know what tomorrow is?"

"Sure I do. It's Thanksgiving, and we have much to be thankful for. Namely, Preston Gordon Hatcher, the second, and Zachary Clayton Richards, Junior!"

"Are you happy, Win?" Mercita asked him.

"Happier than I've ever been in my whole life! Now, let's go and see how our two new mothers are doing."

He knocked on the hospital room door.

"Come in," two happy voices responded cheerfully.

❁

That night Ray and Zachary visited with the new mothers and their newborn sons. After awhile both new mothers decided that they needed to rest, so the men left with specific instructions to be on time for their discharges the next day.

"We're two lucky chaps, you know, Ray," Zachary said as the two walked down the hospital corridor.

"I know, you're so right man. Lucky is right."

"And you know why, don't you, Ray?"

"I have some idea, but what do you think?"

"I believe it's your mother, Ray. She is a very extraordinary woman who kept her courage, her pride in herself, her strength of purpose, her deep sense of responsibility to her family, and she has passed those values on to us. You, me, Ariadne, even your wife, Kendra. We owe her big time. Love and respect for one another, her family, that's what she's given us. I, for one, promise to do my best to continue that precept in my little family."

"Me, too, Zack, me, too," Ray said as they walked to their cars in the hospital's parking lot.

They reached Ray's car first. He stopped beside it, placed his hand on his brother-in-law's arm.

"You know, Zack, my mother was always the most important person in my life, but now I have even more. I have a real family. Mother's given me my father, my heritage, my belonging. My dad's coming into my life to claim me as his has eased my soul. And Mother did it, you know. She made us 'family'."

"I agree," Zack said, aware of all the difficulties Ray had endured. "The family is the basis for all societies, you know. So, aren't we the lucky ones! See you tomorrow, Ray, when we pick up our families!"

"Goin' to be a great day, Zack. See you tomorrow, Thanksgiving, and we certainly have much to be thankful for."

"Amen to that," Zachary agreed. "Amen to that."

Mildred Riley is ninety years young and a natural born storyteller. A retired nurse, she lives in Massachusetts and is delighted with her second career. She currently considering flying lessons.